A ROOM ON LORELEI STREET

A ROOM ON
LORELEI STREET

MARY E. PEARSON

HENRY HOLT AND COMPANY · NEW YORK

So many thanks . . .

to Amanda Jenkins, Catherine Atkins, Gail Giles, Nancy Werlin, Shirley Harazin, and Laura Wiess, for being so generous with their time, insights, advice, and encouragement; and to Jill Rubalcaba for pushing me to begin and then being there from start to finish. Her expertise, support, and creative nagging got me through.

My gratitude to Rosemary Stimola for finding me the perfect match. And deepest thanks to Kate Farrell, for her gentle guidance and for loving Zoe as much as I do.

And always, my everything to Dennis. He makes it all happen.

Henry Holt and Company, LLC, *Publishers since 1866*
175 Fifth Avenue, New York, New York 10010
www.henryholtchildrensbooks.com

Henry Holt® is a registered trademark of Henry Holt and Company, LLC.
Copyright © 2005 by Mary E. Pearson. All rights reserved.
Distributed in Canada by H. B. Fenn and Company Ltd.

Library of Congress Cataloging-in-Publication Data
Pearson, Mary (Mary E.)
A room on Lorelei Street / Mary E. Pearson.—1st. ed.
p.   cm.
Summary: To escape a miserable existence taking care of her alcoholic mother,
seventeen-year-old Zoe rents a room from an eccentric woman, but her earnings as
a waitress after school are minimal and she must go to extremes to cover expenses.
ISBN-13: 978-0-8050-7667-7
ISBN-10: 0-8050-7667-0
1. Freedom—Fiction.   2. Family problems—Fiction.   3. Interpersonal
relations—Fiction.   4. Alcoholism—Fiction.   5. Lodging houses—Fiction.
6. Texas—Fiction.]   I. Title.
PZ7.P32316Ro   2005   [Fic]—dc22   2004054015

First Edition—2005 / Designed by Donna Mark
Printed in the United States of America on acid-free paper. ∞

10   9   8   7   6   5   4   3   2

". . . but you excel them all."

For Helen and Dorothy,
with my love and thanks

A ROOM ON LORELEI STREET

ONE

It used to be a house.

You could almost have called it pretty.

She stares at chain-link threaded with weeds, a few of them blooming. Her vision blurs on white petals and regains focus on a patch of lawn the fence holds in—or what might have been a lawn once. She can't remember that it has ever been green but knows it once was more than the dusty stubble it is now. She thinks about the rough texture between her toes, running across it, barefoot, with the hot Texas sun pressing down from above and a cool, lazy sprinkler refreshing from below. She remembers a six-year-old girl whose laughter came easy. She remembers but wonders, Was it ever really that way?

No pretense is made of throwing out a sprinkler now. It is not a house anymore. She knows that. The only life is in the weeds that live in the protection of the chain-link.

She throws down her cigarette and mashes it on the sidewalk, kicking it over with a pile of a dozen others. She breathes out one last, smoke-filled breath and almost smiles. There is still a little pretense left. She slips a peppermint into her mouth and lifts the latch of the gate. It groans, low and heavy, whispering, *Don't go in. Don't go in.*

But she does.

TWO

"Mama?"

The front room is heavy with the smell of dusty furniture and stale cigarettes. She walks to the kitchen and sees a plate of eggs and buttered toast, untouched, still sitting at the kitchen table where she left it this morning. She shoves aside dishes, unopened mail, and brimming ashtrays, and sets her books on the counter.

"Mama?" she calls again.

There is no answer.

The floor beneath her creaks as she walks down the short hallway. The first door is open, the room dark. Her hand slides around the wall and flips on the light. The room is empty, but she yanks back the shower curtain just to be sure.

She has to be sure.

The bathtub is empty, the glimmering white a macabre gift, and a faint, strangled noise escapes through her throat as she turns off the light and continues down the hall. The door opposite her own is closed, but she turns the knob and slivers it open, just enough to see bare legs across rumpled sheets and a never-made bed. Heavy breathing, the sound of deep slumber, drifts out of the room along with the smell of hair spray, oily linen, and anisette. She closes the door, shutting in the smells and sounds, and steps across the hall to her own room. The air is hot and still.

She hits the switch on her fan to high and scans the room. *What should I take? What?* She grabs a duffel bag from beneath her bed and begins to fill it. Jeans, underwear, T-shirts, pajamas, the blanket from her bed? There isn't room for it all. She empties the bag and starts over, trying to decide what must go. When the duffel is full, her pillowcase is stuffed with more. Her ragged Eeyore, headphones, a framed picture of her and Kyle, her broken jewelry box with the plastic ballerina. She steps back and stares at the duffel bag and bulging pillowcase lying on her bed. Full and waiting. Stares at them for four minutes, imagining them resting on a different bed—a bed in a room, down a hall, in a house, on a street named Lorelei.

Lorelei.

A pretty name. What does it mean? Maybe a flower. Maybe a sparkling, rushing river in a faraway part of the world. She whispers it aloud, "Lorelei." The sound makes her ache, makes the word even more beautiful, even more real. Her eyes close, and her hands inch up to hug her arms.

The only sound is the whirring and chink of the fan as it oscillates back and forth. *Lorelei.* The fan whirs and whispers again and again, *Lorelei, Lorelei, Lorelei.*

Whir.

    Chink.

Her eyelids flutter open. This is not Lorelei Street. She unzips the duffel. Piece by piece, everything is put back exactly where it had been. The same with the pillowcase, until it only holds a limp, beaten-down pillow. Her eyes lock onto the deflated case for another silent minute and then she goes to the kitchen to wash dishes and throw forgotten eggs down the disposal.

The dishwasher is broken—it has been for months—so she fills the sink with hot water and squirts in dish soap. Soft bubbly water rises, enveloping cereal-crusted bowls, coffee cups with smeared lines of lipstick, and glasses with burgundy-colored stains. They are swallowed by the white bubbles, erasing three more days and promising a fresh start. *A fresh start.* Again, she almost smiles and dips her fingers into the hot water searching for the sponge.

"Hey, sugar."

She turns and sees Mama leaning against the doorway, still rubbing sleep from her eyes. Mama is pretty, striking, even as she is now. She looks at Mama's legs, each day growing thinner, taut, the knees protruding like bony knobs while her trunk bloats like a barrel. Her eyes are puffy, her shimmering white-blond hair, brittle. But still, Mama is beautiful, delicate and light like a fragile china doll.

"I thought you were going to work today, Mama," she says, turning back to the sink, searching for the sponge hidden beneath the bubbles. She finds it and vigorously scrubs the first glass.

"I called and there weren't any appointments for me."

There haven't been appointments in weeks. No one wants Mama anymore. Her hands shake, and Mama talks about things no one wants to hear. The glass is clean, but she continues to scrub. "There's always walk-ins. Sally always has walk-ins for you."

"I just wasn't up to it. Not feeling too well. I—"

"You didn't eat the eggs I made you. You said you would. Before I left for school you said—"

Mama leaves. She walks from the kitchen to the front room, brushes week-old newspapers from the couch to the floor, and lies down. "Come on in here, sugar. I'll get those dishes later. Come sit with me and talk."

Talk. She rinses the glass and feels her stomach squeeze. There will be no *talk*. Only listening. And listening.

I can't. Not anymore. Not one more sentence, one more word, one more breath, or I will explode. I will die. It's been said before. All of it. Again and again. Not one more word. Not one.

She dries the glass swirling the towel over and over, around and around, till it squeaks, pleading for a breath, and then she dries it again. "I can't," she whispers, so lightly the sound is lost behind the humming refrigerator and the squeaking of the dry glass.

"Sugar?"

She stops drying and slips the glass back into the soapy bubbles. "Coming, Mama."

Mama talks, and she listens. There is no explosion, no suffocating, no dying—just listening and listening to stories and retellings she has memorized. She adds a word here and there, because Mama needs her to.

"Mama, it will be okay."

"Mama, that was in the past."

"Mama, don't cry."

Mama. Mama. Mama. It's always about Mama.

She glances at her watch. Her shift at the diner starts in an hour.

Mama finally remembers. "Oh. Today was your first day. How did it go?"

She looks at Mama's hand curled around her own. It is warm and soft. "I got the classes I wanted. Not all the teachers, but I did get the classes. Sixth-period P.E., too, so I can go straight to tennis."

"You're taking tennis?"

"After school, Mama. I'm on the team. I already told you." She's been on the team for two years. Mama has never seen her play.

"Oh, that's right. I forgot." Mama begins to drift, her eyes half closed.

There is more about her day that Mama should know. Should she tell? A smile plays behind her eyes, comes nowhere near her mouth—the pretense is there again—Mama still signs the notes, is still on the parent information card at school.

"There is one other thing. You might be getting a phone call—from the principal."

Mama's eyes open. "On the *first* day, sugar?"

She sees the clarity she yearns for.

"It was a cussword, Mama. Just one little cussword that slipped out before I knew it. It didn't mean anything."

"Is that all? One little word? Don't worry. I'll talk to the principal. He'll forget all about it." Mama rolls to her side and closes her eyes.

She thinks about fifth period. American Lit. The principal won't forget. She tries to remember exactly how it happened. Was it the afternoon sun? The rising temperature and over-crowded classroom? Going without a cigarette all day? Or was it the way Mrs. Garrett looked too much like Grandma when she tilted her head? Too much like Grandma when she looked down her nose over half glasses while calling roll but never once bothering to look into a single face in the class-room? Or maybe it was the muffled laughter that rolled through the room when Mrs. Garrett called her name. . . .

"Zo?" Mrs. Garrett calls.

A sprinkling of laughter. And then, like it amuses her, like an encore performance, Mrs. Garrett calls again. Slowly this time, louder, so she owns the name. "Zo?"

It isn't exactly a snap. More like a simmer with steadily increasing heat.

"Zoe," she corrects.

And then the simmer grows hotter and she stands.

"Zz—o—eeee."

A nervous, hushed titter runs through the classroom.

"Zo—eeeee," she says again, to be sure she is clear. She has to be clear. "Got it?" she finally asks.

"Oh . . . *yes,*" Mrs. Garrett says, setting aside the roll sheet and looking over her glasses in a classroom where there is no air to breathe. "I got it."

But the answer doesn't seem enough. Her mind reaches full boil.

How the hell could a know-it-all English teacher not know how to pronounce Zoe? Zoe, for God's sake! Where did she get her degree from? She can expel my sorry ass from here to Abilene, but she sure as hell is going to get my name right. She's going to know how to pronounce my name. My name. Zoe.

She steps closer, her feet pushing her to the front of the classroom like in a dream.

"Zoe," she says. "Zoe . . . *with a loud, fucking* E," she tells Mrs. Garrett. And when she says it, it isn't a whisper.

+ *
 +

Zoe stands, releasing Mama's limp hand, and thinks it probably wasn't the heat or the cigarettes or the overcrowded classroom at all. *Zoe,* she thinks, and then says it aloud to make it more real. "Zoe." But the breathless little word is lost in a room of dust and clutter, because Mama is asleep, and there is no one else to hear.

THREE

She rolls down the window of her blue Thunderbird and speeds through the streets of Ruby. A smile spreads across her face when she thinks about fifth period. She is dead. Mrs. Garrett, of *all* teachers, the teacher who instills fear in the hearts of incoming freshmen and sends seniors flocking to the counseling office for transfers when her name appears on their schedules. *Mrs. Garrett.* What was she thinking?

But who knows? Maybe this *once* Mama will take care of it like she promised.

"Zoe!" she screams out the window and laughs.

Zoe. She likes her name. Her father gave it to her. He specially chose it for the unseen life growing in her mother's stomach. Aunt Patsy told her. She spilled the beans to Zoe one day when she was angry at Mama. She told her what no one else would. She told her what Daddy said. Seventeen years ago, they were all jammed into Grandma's tiny living room—Aunt Patsy, Uncle Clint, Aunt Nadine with her new baby sucking at her breast, Grandma, and of course Mama and Daddy. It wasn't a private conversation as it should have been, but nothing in the Buckman family ever was. "You can't get rid of it, Darlene," he said. "There's already a precious life growing in there. I bet it's a little girl as beautiful as you. I'm gonna give her a name right now. Zoe. That means 'life.' You can't just flush away life."

Grandma was spitting mad. She hated Daddy, and she hated the name Zoe, but Mama went along with it because she loved the man who was patting her flat tummy. Mama made a choice and held tight to it. They were married a week later. When the next baby came along six years later, Grandma picked the name. Kyle Broderick Buckman. And Mama went along with that because she loved Grandma, too.

Zoe switches on her blinker to turn and wonders why her aunt told her the secret. She and Mama used to be best friends. That's how Aunt Patsy met Uncle Clint, Mama's older brother. Aunt Patsy seemed like she loved and hated Mama all at the same time—one minute making excuses for her and the next telling secrets that Grandma worked hard to keep.

Zoe turns left at the corner of Redmond and Main—the opposite direction from Murray's Diner—but she has her detour timed. She knows she won't be late. She has taken the same route six times now and has never been as much as a second late punching in at the restaurant. She has never been late. She never plans to be. Being on time is important.

Any first-grader knows that, she thinks.

The thought weaves into her unexpectedly, as so many thoughts do, time and again. *How do you make the remembering stop?* The shame is fresh, like it has been circling through her veins all along and on a whim has decided to burn hotly again. Being six years old and ashamed that she is not remembered. Getting dark. And darker. Six years old, alone, waiting to be picked up. She adjusts the sash of her Brownie uniform, turns, moves like she is busy. Like she knows someone will come soon. The appearance at least lightens the shame. Maybe the Brownie leader watching won't know she is forgotten. The tightness in her chest grows. The tightness that says, *You are alone, Zoe.* No one remembers you are at Brownies. Mama had insisted. She said Zoe had to join. It would be fun. But Zoe hates it. She hates the pity as she sews button eyes on a puppet with a borrowed mom. Mama didn't know about that. That moms came, too. At least sometimes. And they remembered to pick up their daughters.

Zoe checks her watch again, creating what she craves, the dependability that she knows can exist if you care enough. That's all it takes. An ounce of caring.

About half a mile down Main she turns right onto Carmichael. It takes her into a neighborhood of old homes and deep parkways planted with huge, twisted fig trees that have turned the nearby sidewalk into a patchwork of uprooted planes of concrete. She is surprised she never drove through this neighborhood before last week. Ruby is a small town. The sign as you enter claims a population of 9,500. Nestled between the smaller towns of Duborn to the east and Cooper Springs to the west, it ups the whole population of the area to maybe 15,000. You can drive through it all, end to end, in fifteen minutes.

She wonders how she could have missed this neighborhood. She has lived all her life in Ruby. She has been left to stay the night at more houses than she can remember when Mama and Daddy forgot to come pick her up—houses of friends who never lived on a street like hers. She has slept with half a dozen boys in as many houses, all in neighborhoods far from her own. She has visited classmates' homes and crashed parties, but nothing ever brought her down Carmichael Street until Murray asked her to deliver a rhubarb pie to his dad. "The old man's crankier than hell, and Mom's hoping that the sugar will send him into a diabetic coma and give her a little peace."

Zoe appreciates Murray's humor. She knows his dad. He comes in most Saturday mornings for hash browns and weak tea. He is a gentle, stooped man with a wobbly voice and an unstable gait, who announces his arrival by jingling the change in his pocket. Murray always saves the corner seat at the counter for him. He comes in less these days—his health failing—but Murray still saves the seat, just in case.

"No problem, Murray," she had said and left with the

pie. She didn't pay attention to the neighborhood overly much on her way. She delivered the pie to Murray's parents and then headed for home. *Home.* Walls, floors, unpaid bills, dirty dishes, Mama, and nothing more. *Home.* Mama would either be unconscious or want to talk. *Home.*

Her mind bobbed and weaved around the word, what it meant and what she wanted it to mean, so she didn't notice the fig trees, the shaded parkways, the crumpled sidewalks, or the old but loved homes. She didn't notice any of it until a tiny red sign high in a window wedged its way into her life.

She turns off Carmichael onto the street whose name replays in her head over and over again, a background beat that everything else melts into. Six houses down she pulls her car to a stop at the uneven curb. She opens her door, then eases it closed behind her, careful not to slam it, severing the silence and maybe the dream.

She walks around and leans against the blue car that she has come to call her own. Mama can't drive because her license is suspended, so the Thunderbird has become Zoe's. The chrome digs into her back and she shifts, but she won't leave her viewpoint. She can't. Mama herself has pinned her to this place. Daddy, too. Pinned and pushed with years of so much . . . nothing.

One house away she can see the tiny red sign in the upper window. She checks each day on her way to work, and each day it is still there. Each day, she leans against her car and imagines what the house is like inside—*what the room is like*. The house is old, so the room must be old, the floors probably polished wood, a staircase that's worn, with a smooth, burnished banister, perhaps teeth marks where a child has chewed it. A braided blue rug rests at the top of the stairs. A calico cat curls around a chest of drawers and disappears into a doorway. Carefully chosen paintings hang on the walls, and maybe pictures of family, too. Old pictures. Loved pictures. There are probably smells in the house, too. Smells she would like. Lavender. Blueberry muffins. Freshly squeezed lemons. Cleanser. Polish. She can almost hear a washing machine, churning, churning, washing away all the dirt that a house can hold. A radio plays lightly in the kitchen and jangled, cheerful humming comes from some other room in the house. What else would be in a house like that? She allows herself fifteen minutes every day to think about it.

Beyond the short wooden fence that surrounds the property she has seen a woman stooped in the garden. The woman is old, small, and delicate-boned. Her hair is wild and her clothes mismatched. Today she is not there. Zoe wonders if she is a worker or maybe the owner of the house—the owner of the room.

Her eyes are still turned in the direction of the house, but she no longer sees it. Instead she sees her pay stubs and adds them up. With tips she brings home about $210 every two weeks; monthly that's $420. Knock off forty dollars for gas—what does she spend on cigarettes? Twenty, thirty dollars? She isn't sure, so she will say thirty. About forty a week for groceries—times four is $160 a month. Lunches and other incidentals probably add up to another thirty dollars? She concentrates, trying to add it in her head. "Two-sixty," she whispers. That leaves $160. She has little saved, maybe two hundred hidden in her drawer at home, and that is because she just got paid. *Where does it all go?*

Mama.

Mama always forgets to pay a bill and needs a little help. "Sugar, just run down to the utility office with some cash, will you? I'll pay you back. I'm a little short." But Mama always seems to find the money for other things.

Zoe continues to work with her figures. She could cut back on her cigarettes and eat more at Murray's. She should be able to come up with $180 left over. One hundred eighty. It sounds like so much, but—

"You going to stand there, or you going to come up and take a look?"

Zoe jumps, her cigarette tumbling from her fingers into the gutter. Pay stubs and figures disappear from her vision, and she focuses on the person who appeared out of nowhere. A brown grocery bag is in her arms.

"Excuse me?" she says to the wild-haired woman she saw in the garden five days ago.

"I've seen you here three or four times now. Guessed you were checking out the neighborhood. You must've figured out by now that we don't have any roving gangs around here—a couple folks whose cheese has slid off their cracker, but that's about it. So, you ready to see the room?"

Zoe thinks the old lady's voice doesn't match her attitude. She is assertive, almost snippy, confident in a crazy, old-woman way, but she is smiling, and her voice is soft, lyrical. It reminds Zoe of a bird.

"Is it your room?"

The old lady snorts. "My house. So I guess it must be my room, too. Here. Let's go." She shoves the bag of groceries into Zoe's arms and starts walking. Zoe follows.

"But I really don't have time. . . ." Zoe tries to turn her wrist so she can see her watch, but the groceries prevent her. What is she doing? "Ma'am?"

But the lady keeps walking. Down the sidewalk, up the drive, around to a side walkway, finally stopping at the bottom of a narrow stairway that hugs the side of the garage. She raises her foot to the first step and turns to Zoe.

"Has its own entrance so you can come and go when you want—you keep crazy hours?"

Zoe hesitates, trying to decide. Is midnight crazy on a weeknight? She doesn't think so. Weekends are different, but she could change that.

"No, not too crazy."

"Too bad. I'm up all hours—never could keep a schedule." She chuckles, and takes another step up.

"Wait!" Zoe stops her. "Shouldn't I find out how much first? That is, what you're asking for the room?"

The lady turns, and combs her wild corkscrew wisps back with her fingers. "Two hundred a month," she says.

In an instant, Zoe feels the heavy, stale air of the hallway sweep over her and sees rumpled, dirty sheets. She smells the cold, never-eaten eggs in the kitchen and the sweet stench of burgundy-stained glasses drowning in soap bubbles. She knows she needs to say something, but no words come.

The lady slaps her hand on the stair rail like she has just remembered something. "Leastways, that's what I *was* asking, but seeing as I haven't had any takers, I'm having a blow-out sale—today it goes for one-fifty. That includes utilities and a plot in the garden."

A sale? One-hundred fifty? That would leave her with thirty dollars to spare. A finger of wind ruffles Zoe's hair and she smells the autumn crocus breezing up from the garden.

FOUR

The lady rummages through her pocket for the key. "I still have a few things in there, but I can take them out if they don't ka-nish with your ka-nash." She slides the key into the lock, and the door swings open. Zoe steps inside. The old lady takes the groceries from her arms and sets them on a small half-circle table next to the door. "This is it," she says.

Zoe's arms prickle. She turns, trying to take it all in. A dull ache grows in her chest. It is not for her. It is too much. A real room with real floors and walls. A room for sleeping and reading and dancing and . . . in her imagination she has pictured the room, but she has never seen herself in it.

Her shoes squeak as she turns on the polished wooden floors. The room takes up the whole space over the garage. On the opposite wall is a jukebox showing signs of age, parts of its chrome grill mottled with black and green splotches, with real 45s lining the back, waiting to be pulled forward by a poised mechanical arm. Next to it is a bed, a large four-poster with wood so dark it is nearly black, like the old oiled pews at Ruby First Baptist. The mattress is white-tufted bareness, waiting for someone . . . *someone* to cover it with a spread.

Her eyes continue to scan the room. A large-paned window that looks out on the street and driveway fills the room with shafts of late-afternoon light. A deep window seat with a hodgepodge of worn, colorful pillows lies below it. To the right is an old wooden dresser, the same coffee-black color as the four-poster bed. It holds a large brass clock in the shape of a panther, the time ticking away across its belly. The clock is reflected in the ornate carved mirror behind it, so two panthers creep in unison across the dark dresser. The reflection in the mirror draws Zoe's eyes to the ceiling for the first time. She leans her head back to take it all in. It is deep indigo blue, like a rich velvet blanket to keep everything underneath safe and warm. It is as deep and dark as the Ruby sky on a moonless night. She can barely see faint luminescent spots scattered across the blue expanse. Stars, she thinks. This crazy, corkscrew-haired lady has painted stars on her ceiling.

She lowers her gaze and continues around the room. In the corner, to the right of the entrance is a makeshift kitchenette, obviously new and added on. It has a tiny refrigerator, a small sink with a narrow tiled counter, and a huge wooden hutch that holds a hot plate and a coffeemaker.

"What do you think?" the lady asks.

She wants to say it is magnificent. She wants to run over to the bed and jump up and down on the mattress like a ten-year-old, reaching up to touch the ceiling and the stars and screaming and laughing, *I will take it, I will take it,* but she knows she needs to say something else.

"It's nice," she says. "Why are you renting it out?" She is glad her words come out calm and even, like she has done this before, like she knows what to ask when she doesn't.

The old lady's eyes meet Zoe's, and for the first time Zoe notices their color—clear light amber with flecks of faded green. "Fair question," the lady says as she pulls a package of red licorice from the grocery bag and rips it open. She offers a strand to Zoe then takes one for herself. "My tax man suggested it. Said it's a way to 'defray costs,' a fancy way of saying it will help make ends meet. Guess he's right. The damn house has been paid off for years, but taxes and licorice keep going up, and Social Security doesn't."

"Oh," Zoe says like she understands. Taxes. She twists the red cord in her fingers. She only wanted to make sure no one had been murdered in this room. It seemed like a reasonable thought, but now it is ridiculous, childish. A new feeling is spreading through her. Like there are too many things that she needs to understand but doesn't. Will she have to pay taxes? *Shit. Why am I here?*

"The bathroom is through there," the lady says, pointing

to a door next to the jukebox. "The kitchen wasn't too diffi-cult, but a bathroom was just too hard to add. It's in with the rest of the house—just down the hall, and you have it all to yourself. That a problem?"

A problem? Zoe doesn't know. It suddenly seems like too big of a decision. A bathroom down the hall? Her excitement mixes with fear and she can't think. She doesn't know what to say. *What do you think, Zoe? What? What?* She takes a bite of licorice to give herself more time to think. She chews and swallows. "No, I don't think it's a problem," she says, but she is not sure if that is what she wanted to say at all.

"Opal," the lady says holding out her hand. "Opal Keats."

Zoe takes her hand and feels papery skin and wiggling veins beneath her fingers. The hand is warm and small in her own. "Zoe Beth Buckman," she says.

Opal smiles and twists her head to the side like a spar-row, as if she is trying to get a better view of her. "You old enough to be renting a place, Zoe?" she asks.

Zoe thinks. She is seventeen years old . . . going on a hundred. She changed more of Kyle's diapers than Mama and Daddy put together. She has cleaned vomit from the bathroom floor more times than she can remember and has washed her own clothes since she was ten. She has tucked Mama into bed and kissed her forehead but can't remember when Mama's lips last brushed her own temple as she went to sleep. She has worked since she was twelve, first baby-sitting, then waiting tables. She identified Daddy at the morgue when Mama was too broken up and Grandma couldn't be bothered. She has lived at least three lifetimes in her seventeen years. She looks into Opal's eyes. "Yes," she says. "I'm old enough."

"I can see that now," Opal says, squinting. "I can see it in your eyes. You have an old soul." There is a long pause. Silence. Not even the panther clock seems to make a sound. Zoe turns around once more, taking a last look at the room, seeing details she missed before, like the braided rug at the end of the bed and a life-size stone bulldog tucked under the table by the front door. She hears her thick rubber-soled waitress shoes squeak on the floor as she turns and then remembers that this was how she imagined it. Polished wooden floors. That much she knew.

"Will you be taking the room, Zoe?" Opal asks.

Zoe pulls her car keys from her pocket. She looks every-where but into Opal's eyes. She aches for the room, but a weight, a whisper, pulls at her. . . . *What about Mama . . . what about Mama?* She reaches down and brushes the head of the stone bulldog. "I'll have to think on it," she says, and she leaves not caring that, for the first time ever, she will be late for work.

FIVE

Zoe stops the car at the curb and turns off the ignition, but she doesn't get out. It was a busy night at the diner and she is tired, more tired than she should be after a short shift. Instead of thinking on it as she promised Opal, she had tried to concentrate on other things, like orders of chicken-fried steak or peach cobbler, even school and Mrs. Garrett. All through her shift she battled to keep the room out of her head—the room she couldn't possibly take—but instead the battle escalated into a raging war.

"You okay?" Murray asked her when a plate of fries and a patty melt crashed from her arm to the floor.

"Yes," she said, but even as she helped clean up the mess, all she could see was a clock on a brass panther's belly, ticking away seconds, months, and years.

No peace is in sight, but she desperately needs some. She kicks off her shoes, rolls down the window of the Thunderbird and leans her seat back. She can't go into the house. She still needs a few moments alone. Time.

It's a hot September night, but heat has never bothered Zoe. She hears Mr. Kalowatz's sprinklers hissing next door, and from across the street a faint drone from the Fensters' TV drifts through their screen door. It is so still, so calm, she thinks, and she drinks it in. Periodically a tree frog starts up a wave of chirping and then quiets again. And that she soaks in, too. All those things outside of herself that seem to have order. She lets them seep in.

For a moment she forgets and is able to fall into the stillness. The gentle harmony of sounds cradles her, rocks her, and in the darkness, her tired faded house seems almost beautiful. She rubs her stocking feet together to push away the soreness and looks out the window into the glittered sky.

The angels threw glitter up there just for you, Zoe, Daddy had told her. *They celebrated almost as much as I did the day you were born. Every time you look up there you remember how special you are—so special the angels threw a big party.*

She rests her head on the ledge of the window and scans the billions of blinking stars sprinkled all the way down to the horizon. *A party,* she thinks. "I must have been pretty special, Daddy," she whispers. The Hendersons' dog two houses down begins barking, which starts a domino effect, and distant dogs throughout the neighborhood join in, until the sprinklers, the reruns of *M*A*S*H*, and even the shrill tree frog are a background rhythm. She smiles at how quickly calm can turn to chaos. Mr. Henderson comes out his door and yells for his dog to shut up, and soon the dog's silence begins a reverse domino effect. The crescendo subsides, and the calm returns. It's all connected in strange, mysterious ways, she guesses . . . the sprinklers, the *M*A*S*H* reruns, the tree frog, the dogs, even Mr. Henderson . . . all connected in ways they can't ever know, ways only she can sense, because on this dark, starry night she is there to hear them. She is there to listen.

Almost revived, she gathers her shoes and purse to go into the house—and to Mama. The chain-link gate groans its usual warning as she passes through, and she tries to ignore it. *I have to go in,* she thinks. When she reaches the steps, she sees a red tag hanging on the doorknob and she squeezes her eyes tight, trying to hold the battle in. She snatches the notice from the door and reads that they have forty-eight hours left before the power is cut.

"Dammit, Mama!" she says under her breath as she opens the door. "Mama?" she calls. There is no answer. She walks to the kitchen and sees a gallon jug of red wine sitting on the table, half its contents already gone. She slaps the notice onto the table next to the jug. The dishes from this afternoon still sit in the sink, now covered with cold, gray water.

"When *is* 'later,' Mama?" she sighs. She turns to go to her room, but a scrap of paper taped to the refrigerator catches her eye.

*Sorry, Sugar. Principal called. Had his mind set so I
didn't even try. No big deal. One-day suspension. Go
to counselor's office in the morning. Something about
counseling during sixth period on Fridays, too. Sounds
cushy and gets you out of class.*

Mama

Zoe feels a hot rush in her chest. *Yes, Mama, it is a big
deal! I have P.E. sixth period! Tennis! But it will be a cold day in
hell before you ever remember that!* She rips the note from the
refrigerator. "Mama!" she calls. She walks down the hall,
past the bathroom, to Mama's closed door. The note trembles in one hand, and she opens the door with the other.
She stops when it is only open a few inches.

Mama's legs lie tangled in the sheets, but between them
two larger, hairier legs move in a rhythm that make Zoe's
stomach wrench. She stumbles back from the door, leaving
it ajar and fumbles for her own doorknob, searching for an
escape. She falls into her room, closing the door behind her.

Zoe feels her breath coming fast, out of control. A flash
of sweat heats her face. *She can't even be bothered to lock
her door. She doesn't think that, maybe for me, she should lock her
lousy fucking door.* She stands in the middle of her dark room
with her hands over her face, pressing, measuring breaths
that want to come in gulps, pressing to hold it in. *That's
where the wine came from. She won't do one stinking thing for
me, but for that she will screw her way to oblivion.*

Zoe falls onto her bed in the dark and pulls her pillow over her face. Her gulping breaths are muffled. The only other sound is the jingling of her tips as they slip from her skirt pocket to the floor. The pillow is wet against her face, and her uneven breaths pull something out of her she hates, pulling until her head throbs and a sharp stab swells in her throat. Finally her breathing quiets and she lies on her back, limp, staring into the blackness, her chest occasionally jumping for a breath like it did when she was a child. The darkness vibrates around her and the room is stuffy, but she is too weak to get up and turn on the light or the fan. She wishes the black void would swallow her up. It would be easier.

Her chest jumps again, and she thinks of Kyle and how she used to rub his chest when he was little and hold him tight in her arms so the shaking would go away. "It will be all right, Kiteman," she would whisper against his cheek, no matter what the problem was, whether it was a scraped knee, or it was a lonely, stormy night and Mama and Daddy still hadn't come home. She always promised him everything would be all right.

But it's not.

What does he think of her now?

Zoe sits up on her bed. She doesn't allow herself to think about Kyle too often. Like Aunt Patsy with Mama, she loves and hates him all at the same time. He's been gone almost two years now. When Daddy died it was decided that Mama couldn't handle nine-year-old "boy energy" for a while. He would go stay with Aunt Patsy and Uncle Clint—just till Mama got over it. It was only supposed to be for a few weeks, but then those few turned into a few more, and then more, and soon everyone seemed to forget that Kyle had ever lived with Mama and Zoe. Even when Aunt Patsy got sick, Kyle stayed. Everyone acted like it was normal, and Zoe stopped asking when he would come back home, because she knew he wouldn't. It was never considered that maybe Zoe should go live with Aunt Patsy and Uncle Clint, too. When Zoe brought it up to Grandma, she frowned and said, "No. Your mama needs you. You need to be here. Besides, there isn't any room for you at Clint and Patsy's."

Zoe leans forward in the darkness, her fingers digging into her face.

No room.

SIX

Zoe sits in a chair in the hallway. Waiting. Mrs. Farantino is expecting her, the secretary says. Zoe leans to the side and peers in the office. It is empty. If Mrs. Farantino is expecting her, where is she? Zoe wonders. Probably in the lounge finishing her bagel and coffee. Zoe comes after bagel and coffee but before potty break. She smiles, wondering if this is how she will have to amuse herself all day—figuring out where she fits in.

Somehow, a one-day suspension doesn't bother her. She has done it before. Last year, for ditching class, she was suspended from class. The irony still amuses her. It's the counseling that nags at her. Mrs. Farantino has known Zoe since she skipped her first class when she was a freshman, but this is the first time formal counseling has been ordered.

The air-conditioning vent above her head rumbles. *Get out of it,* she hears. She will. She is not going to play the spill-your-guts game with anyone. The secretary taps her pencil as she stares at her computer screen. Her desk is a piled mess of papers, pencil cups, and clutter, but Zoe focuses on a small potted plant on the corner. Violets. Fresh, blooming, well-watered violets. She looks away. *Where is she?* Zoe wonders. *How long does one freakin' bagel take?* But Mrs. Farantino still doesn't come.

The violets creep back into her vision. She leans forward, remembers. Bits. Turns. Beginnings. Mama sad. Crying. Days of crying. It began with the potted violets that Daddy forgot to water. They screamed at each other. A glass was broken. Daddy slammed the door. Zoe pulled a kitchen chair over to the sink and filled a cup. She watered the violets on the sill, but they were already dead. Four days later Mama and Daddy are still sad-mad, and Zoe dresses up in the purple flowery dress Aunt Nadine sent her for her seventh birthday. She dances around the room. She tries to make them smile, desperate tiptoe dancing because she wants to make it better. *Wanting.* Always that. An almost-there kind of hope that keeps her swirling and twirling. But the dead violets on the windowsill are the only flowers that matter. Zoe wishes she had noticed. She should have. She should have watered the violets. *What if she had?*

"Come on in, Zoe." Mrs. Farantino catches Zoe by surprise, briskly turning a corner and walking straight into her office. Zoe follows and waits to be told where to sit. There are four chairs. Zoe looks at one in the far corner. Mrs. Farantino points to a chair close to her own and Zoe sits.

Mrs. Farantino flips through some paperwork while Zoe looks around the room. Posters of smiling teens fill the walls with phrases like "We're in this together" and "One step at a time." *Really*, Zoe thinks.

The room is cluttered with stacks of papers, greeting cards haphazardly tacked to the walls, boxes of books, two backpacks lying on the floor in the corner, and Post-it notes placed all around the edges of the computer and along the ledge of a bookcase. Mrs. Farantino is one of three counselors at Ruby High. She counsels students with last names *A* through *H*. Zoe knows she could have done worse. She is grateful her name doesn't begin with the letter *T*. Mr. Hanford is the counselor for those students—and he's also Mrs. Garrett's brother-in-law. Sometimes Ruby is way too small.

Mrs. Farantino sets aside her file. "So, do you want to tell me what happened?" she asks.

"You already know."

"But I want to hear it from your viewpoint."

"Will that change anything? Will my suspension go away?"

Mrs. Farantino sits back in her chair. She is silent.

I got her, Zoe thinks.

"We need to talk about this, Zoe" she says. Her eyes fix on Zoe and won't let go.

Zoe doesn't want to talk, but the Friday counseling session still nips at her. Fridays are important. She wants that extra practice time to warm up before the after-school practice. She needs that edge since she doesn't have private tutors like so many of the girls on the team do. But talk is cheap, she decides. It will cost her nothing but a chunk of her soul.

"I told Mrs. Garrett how to pronounce my name."

Mrs. Farantino doesn't move. Doesn't speak.

So I used the word fuck, Zoe thinks. She hears people say it a thousand times a day. No one notices. Pass the fuckin' fries, look at this fuckin' book, hand me the fuckin' pen. But if the word should fall on Mrs. Garrett's delicate pink ears, all hell breaks loose.

Mrs. Farantino is still quiet.

"I used the word *fuck*," Zoe says. "I don't think Mrs. Garrett liked it."

A hint of a smile pulls at the corner of Mrs. Farantino's mouth and she leans forward. "No. I don't think she 'liked' it." She reaches out and lays her hand on the arm of Zoe's chair. She is so close Zoe can count the lines fanning out from her eyes. "But it was more than just the word, Zoe. You know that, don't you?"

Mrs. Farantino's face is too close to hers. Zoe wants to pull back, so she can look at her shoes, the walls, the Post-it notes on the computer, but there isn't room for her eyes to drift. God, she needs room. Mrs. Farantino's black eyes hold her, pinning her against the chair. *What does she want? I can't breathe,* she thinks, and she pushes up from the chair, stepping to the middle of the room.

"Okay, it was more than just the word. I've met people

like Mrs. Garrett before—people who think they know so damn much about everything—they want to control the whole world, including you, and when they make a mistake they won't admit it no matter what the mistake's doing to you and instead they make you feel more stupid and more worthless when it was really them all along, and if you try to tell them they've made a mistake, you can kiss your miserable ass good-bye because more than anything else in the whole fucking world, they don't want to be told that they're wrong!"

Zoe turns, takes a breath, realizes what she has said, what has burst out of her, what she was trying to hold back. *What a stupid dumb-shit I am.* She tries to backtrack to soften her tirade. She lowers her voice. "Is that what you meant by 'more'?"

Mrs. Farantino is not thrown off and does not hesitate. Zoe sees no signs of shock or disgust on her face. "Yes. I mean, I think we can see that this all stems from some anger that you're nursing. After all, Zoe, it *was* the first day. She mispronounced your name. That's all. Mistakes like that happen a hundred times on the first day."

"Maybe. But Mrs. Garrett also has plenty of attitude."

"So do you."

"Does she have to go for counseling?"

"No."

Figures, Zoe thinks. *People like Mrs. Garrett never have to change.*

Mrs. Farantino lays out all the rules. She is kind, sympathetic, but unbending. When Zoe protests that Fridays are not good for her, Mrs. Farantino offers that Zoe's mother has the option of arranging for private counseling. Her mother will need to come in and discuss it with the counseling office. Zoe can't have Mama come in so she concedes. She takes the paper that says she will agree to go to "Support Group" once a week and signs it: Zoe Beth Buckman. She underlines the *e* in Zoe, knowing a copy will go to Mrs. Garrett. It must be signed by her mother as well in order to get back into class tomorrow. She decides she will go once or twice and then fade out. As she leaves to go to the library, where in-school suspension is being held today, Mrs. Farantino stops her.

"Remember, Zoe, this puts you on probation. Besides needing to keep your grades up, good citizenship is required for all school sports—including tennis."

Zoe nods. They always know where to stab the deepest. She goes to the library, stakes out a seat in the corner, and stares out the window at a spindly maple planted between the buildings that has never had enough sun or water to grow. After Zoe hands over her pass, the library aide ignores her, too busy with stacks of books and packing lists to be bothered with playing warden.

She has no homework yet. Just time and her thoughts. Too many thoughts. The hours trickle by. If not for tennis, she would probably screw school altogether. She isn't the greatest tennis player, but good, ranked fourth on the team. She has been playing since she was nine, though in the early years you could hardly call it playing. She thinks about the first time she saw a tennis game. Daddy had dragged her along to the country club where he had to finish some touch-up work on a painting job. While Daddy worked in the clubhouse, she stayed by the courts and watched the ladies in their white skirts, tan-skinned and golden-haired, leaping across the green concrete like they were unicorns in a meadow. Waiters brought them trays of water and iced tea with little lemon wedges. Zoe figured they must own the whole place to be treated so royally. Their little white skirts looked so dainty and Zoe stood transfixed, with her face mashed into the chain-link until a worker shooed her away and she ran back to Daddy.

"I want to play tennis, too," she told him.

A locker room attendant snickered. Daddy set down his brush and wiped his face with a kerchief from his pocket.

"You'd make a great tennis player, Zoe. The best." And then he hugged her and she didn't care that he got smudges of paint on her face and shorts. After he finished his work, he took her straight to the Wal-Mart in Abilene, an hour away, and bought her a racket they had on special for $7.99, and then, when he took not one but two cans of balls from the shelf, she knew he had to think she would truly be the best.

"What about a skirt?" she asked, because that was really what she wanted in the first place. Wal-Mart didn't carry tennis skirts, so he took her to the girls' department and bought her a little white skirt that Mama shortened when they got home. Sitting in the living room, with Daddy taking the tags off the racket and Mama hemming her skirt, she felt more like a princess than she ever had in her life.

Even Grandma's scoffing at the wastefulness and absurdity of a Buckman prancing around on a tennis court couldn't take away that moment.

"Spending money like it's water," Grandma clucked. "Twenty bucks down the drain and putting fool ideas in a child's head."

Zoe ignored Grandma and nestled in closer to Mama's side, feeling the rhythm as Mama pulled the thread with the needle over and over again—all for Zoe. The living room buzzed with life and hope, Daddy imagining how famous Zoe would become, Mama laughing and saying how pretty she would be, and for those few hours, with Daddy on one side and Mama on the other, she felt like all the planets revolved around Zoe Beth Buckman.

In the months that followed, when Mama was at the beauty shop and Daddy was supposed to be watching her and Kyle, he would take them both to the park two blocks away and drop them off to practice while he went across the street to Lena's Hideaway—"just for an hour to take the parch off," but then he'd be gone twice that. He always brought back handfuls of pretzels and cans of soda, so the long wait was soon forgotten. While Daddy was gone, Kyle threw balls over the ragged net. Occasionally one would actually come in Zoe's direction and she would hit it. After that she would practice bouncing the ball in place on the racket because Kyle was only good for ten minutes' worth of ball throwing. And then, while Kyle dug holes in the dirt with a spoon on the edges of the court, she would practice serving the six balls over the net, run to the other side to gather them all up, and then hit the six back in the other direction. She knew nothing about how tennis was played except that the ladies at the country club had shouted "love" over and over again, so she knew it had to be a very good game.

Daddy had to take the parch off often enough that she got a lot of practice and eventually picked up the rules by watching other people who came to play on the shabby, weed-riddled courts. Her six balls dwindled down to two and lost most of their bounce, but she always wore her white skirt that told everyone she was the center of the universe, at least for one day.

"You can go now. ISS lunch is back in the counseling offices."

Zoe looks up, unsure what the library aide is saying.

"You can go," she repeats. "The lunch bell? Didn't you hear it?"

"No," Zoe answers. She stands, swinging her backpack over her shoulder.

She had heard nothing except the sound of Mama and Daddy imagining her greatness.

SEVEN

Zoe shifts her weight. Her right foot aches. She has been waiting in line at the utility office for ten minutes, and the line hasn't moved. Four people are ahead of her. Every time the door opens, a breeze wafts in, enveloping her in the scent of the man behind her. Without looking, she guesses he probably doesn't believe in bathing or else he pumps septic tanks for a living and she considers letting him go ahead of her in line, but she really doesn't want to wait through one extra person either. She holds her breath the next time she hears the bell on the door ring.

The utility office is in the heart of downtown Ruby, sandwiched between Yen's Donuts and Grueber's Gun Shop. It's small, she supposes, since most folks pay through the mail. But a few, like her, have to pay in cash. Their checks and promises are no good. She listens to the lady at the front of the line now, swearing she mailed them a check and if she pays now they better not cash the check, too, or it will bounce for sure because she is not made out of money, ya know, and maybe she just shouldn't pay at all since it will probably come tomorrow and it was probably their mistake in the first place. She is convincing. Zoe almost believes her. But like the clerk behind the counter, she has heard a lot of excuses, too.

Before Zoe left for school this morning, Mama promised that she was going to the beauty shop today. She pressed the final notice and a twenty-dollar bill into Zoe's hand and said, "Take care of the rest of this, sugar, will you? I'll pay you back. Things are just a little tight right now."

Zoe wonders where the twenty came from, if the man with the hairy legs was so appreciative he chipped in on their electric bill, too.

It's not as if Mama has no money. Grandma manages it and doles out a monthly check from the insurance and settlement money they got when Daddy died. Five thousand from the painters' union and twenty-six thousand from Best Deal Motel where he died. One year's wages was settlement enough for his life, they figured. Grandma made Mama pay off the mortgage first thing. "Only sensible thing to do with a windfall like that," she said, and then added under her breath so Mama couldn't hear, "Something good finally came of a Buckman." But that still left almost eight thousand dollars. Grandma righteously doled it out in small amounts each month like she was giving communion, and Zoe never heard Mama squeak. For the care of Daddy's "surviving minors," Mama also got a small Social Security check each month, but even though Kyle lived with Aunt Patsy and Uncle Clint, Mama kept all the money. All together, with Mama working at the beauty shop, there should have been plenty of money to pay the bills. But Mama didn't work much, not more than a few days a month, if that, and usually just doing shampoos. Zoe guessed that Sally looked for jobs that Mama could still do. Sally had always been good to her and Daddy. Mama hasn't worked in three weeks now. Until Mama promised to go to work this morning, Zoe thought she might never work again.

"I'm growin' moss back here," the man in front of her yells.

"Me too," someone farther back in the line calls.

"Same here," Zoe adds.

The lady at the front turns and glares at the restless hecklers, and the clerk shuffles the paperwork nervously. Zoe wonders if having a gun shop next door adds to her anxiety. The lady counts out the cash, gets a receipt, and stomps off. *Only three more to go,* Zoe thinks, and then the bell rings and she holds her breath once again.

EIGHT

Zoe's car jostles on the loose gravel road as she drives out to the aqueduct. With no tennis practice, no homework, and no shift to work, she has time to fill. She doesn't want to go home yet, and she won't let herself go see the room again. The only landmarks to mark her passage are occasional oil pumps. They dot Ruby like little anchors to hold down the paper-flat landscape. Enclosed by chain-link fence, a lot of the pumps in the heart of town are painted to make them more attractive, most often to resemble a katydid. With their angled arms of steel, they do look like an insect poised to hop, but Zoe has always thought of them as wild horses rounded up from the plains and forced to work in tiny chain-link corrals. Their brown coats are streaked with rust and grime. Their blunt heads raise and lower, straining against iron reins for freedom. As a child she thought if she could just pull away the fence they would turn back into the beautiful horses they really were and escape to the open plains. She had had hope in that power. She grunts now at the childish notion.

She pulls off the gravel road and parks beneath a huge stand of mesquite. She was hoping to see other people. The twins, maybe, or Carly or Reid. Or anyone. She can usually count on someone to come out after school and unwind with a six-pack on the hoods of cars in the shade of the mesquite. And then where the aqueduct travels over the wash and is supported by beams, they walk down to cool their feet in the trickling pond below it, always fresh with water leaking from above. Or, if it's one of those days that weighs on her, she walks on the crossbeams lying on top of the aqueduct. She doesn't know what compels her to do it, but she thinks today is one of those days. She gets out of her car and looks back toward Ruby. No dust trail churns up the dirt road yet. She wonders if she missed everyone because she wasted so much time at the utility office.

She walks up the small incline to the aqueduct, the sandy red soil rasping under her shoes, whispering, *Not today. Not today.* But she can already hear the low rumble of the water, her blood is thin, rushing, and she is pulled to the first crossbeam. She kicks off her sandals and places her left foot on the six-inch metal beam, one foot . . . one foot . . . one step at a time she tells herself. That's all it is.

She looks down at the black-blue water, deceptively calm on the surface, a few ripples and nothing more. But she knows the danger, the bodies that have been found miles downstream where the aqueduct widens again. No one who falls in ever survives; the current is too strong, the pull to the bottom unforgiving. She spreads her arms out for balance, and her right foot steps ahead of the left. Another step. And another. The water rumbles, vibrates, her heart beats madly, and a breeze lifts up from the rush below, tossing her hair across her face. She smooths the wisps back so slowly . . . so gently . . . and extends her arm again. Another step, and another. Eleven steps across to the other side and then she follows the next zigzag back. And now across again. She stops midway. Lowers her arms. Listens. Feels the frightening power of the water below her . . . *and she closes her eyes.*

Just for a second—or a few. She isn't sure.

Closed just long enough that up melts with down and light mixes with dark. Closed just long enough to know how totally alive and frightened she is. So she can feel her breaths, fast, her heartbeat, the sweat trickling at her temple, her shirt clinging to her back, the tingling of her fingertips, her muscles trembling, tensing, the adrenaline pulsing, so she feels with stark clarity the wild rush that she is alive. Alive. And it could all end with the slip of a foot, the rush to become blackness, the chaos, calm, just with the passing of a few seconds. Her lungs filling with a pint of liquid and it is over.

That's how fast it could change.

She opens her eyes, steadies her arms, and continues across, two more beams, measuring, concentrating—

"Zoe." The voice comes hushed, careful and pleading. She can't turn around.

"Zoe," it calls again. "Come off."

She takes two more steps. "I'm fine, Reid," she calls. "I'm fine." She reaches the end of the beam and turns around. There is Reid standing on the dirt near the edge of the aqueduct, frozen, as though a sudden movement, even from his eyes, could push her from the beam. "Besides, I'm a good swimmer," she says. She sees Reid isn't amused. His face is pale against his coal-black hair. He says nothing else, like there is no breath left to carry his words. She pauses for a moment thinner than a wisp, sorry she has made his brows pinch together and his pupils turn to pinpoints, but at the same time it makes her feel giddy with power.

She completes the eight-beam zigzag walk, and when she steps back onto the soil on the other side of the wash, she screams with her hands over her head in triumph. "Zoe! Queen of the beams! Queen over water! Queen over death!" The power intoxicates her. Five minutes of control seems like a lifetime. She runs down the wash to the other side and to Reid.

Reid walks to his truck with her sandals in his hand and opens the back gate. "You're crazy, you know."

She scoots back on the gate and hugs her knees to her chest. "Not really. People do crazier things than that every day."

"I'm not talking about the stuff in the papers."

"Neither am I."

Reid pulls a beer from a grocery sack and flips the tab.

He doesn't offer one to Zoe. He knows she doesn't drink. She's tried it. The taste isn't bad, but she can't get past the smell. It is always beer and vomit. That is all she smells.

She lights a cigarette, inhales deeply, and forcefully blows the smoke back out. "Where's Carly?" she asks.

Reid makes the sweeping gestures that Zoe expects. He is part of the drama crowd at school. "Am I my sister's keeper?" he asks.

"Usually."

Reid grunts. "Not today. She's in deep shit, and I'm keeping my distance. Don't want peripheral grounding."

Zoe smiles and shakes her head. Grounding. So foreign to her. It sounds so young. "Very gallant of you," she says. "What happened?"

"Speeding ticket. Her second one. No keys for Carly for a long time."

"Shit. Where did it happen?"

"The usual. The stretch between Gorman and the refineries. They were right behind the last row of trailers at Sunset Gardens. She asked for it. They're always there."

Zoe shakes her head. That's where they got Carly the last time. Why didn't she learn? But who is she to judge Carly on faulty memory. It seems to be a Ruby staple.

She lies back in the truck, and Reid erupts with a long dramatic belch, then smiles and bows. Zoe tweaks her head to the side and feigns disgust but can't restrain a smile. She loves him like a brother, but she can't forget he was the last one. Carly doesn't know. It still shames her when she thinks of it, and it continues to hang between her and Reid, thin, like a ghost, barely seen in fleeting glimpses, in the shadows, but always there in awkward pauses, brief moments of remembrance—how it was, the intimacy that is now a hazy dream.

"I'll give her a call later," she says.

"Nope. A hundred-and-fifty-dollar ticket means no phone either." Reid lies down beside her on the gate. Together they stare into the weave of color over them, a shifting canopy of white-blue sky and quaking leaves of mesquite as the afternoon wind picks up.

"Well, I'll see her tomorrow at school, then," Zoe says.

"You'll be there? Knew you were suspended today. You were the talk of the school. Everyone's saying they would put up with Garrett all year long if they could have just been in that class yesterday. They're saying they love you in one breath and that you're fucking crazy in the next."

Zoe sighs. "How many times are you going to call me crazy in one day, Reid?"

"You tell me. The day's not over."

She doesn't answer. She wonders herself.

An awkward silence comes between them, and she is aware of his jeans brushing the side of her bare thigh, his head just inches from hers. She sits up and throws her cigarette down on the dirt, then stands to mash out the fading embers. Reid changes the subject, and they talk about trivial things neither one cares about until finally Zoe looks at her watch and says she has to go home.

But she doesn't go straight home. She can't stop herself. She takes a brief detour—a detour down Lorelei Street—a detour that takes only fifteen minutes, fifteen minutes of dreaming and imagining, a detour that is really, now, her only route home.

NINE

The house is silent. She checks Mama's room, and the bed is empty.

She went to work. Like she said. She really went to work.

Zoe goes to the kitchen and puts away the half gallon of milk and Chinese express she picked up on the way home. She clears the table of dishes, newspapers, bottles of antacids and washes away the crumbs, coffee rings, and dabs of grape jelly with a dishcloth that is gray and smells of mildew. The worn but clean Formica tabletop glistens with the dampness of the rag, and that glimmer somehow lifts her spirits. She turns on the radio on top of the refrigerator. Mama has it tuned to an oldies-but-goodies station, and Zoe leaves it there. She listens to Roy Orbison croon "it's over" as she runs hot water to wash a few dishes.

She glances at the clock. Six-fifteen. Mama should be home soon. Sally's closes at seven; the last shampoos are done by six-thirty. It's only three blocks away, which Mama walks now that she can't drive. Zoe pictures Mama's withering legs. *But the exercise is good for her,* she thinks. She finishes the dishes and looks at the empty sink. It is stained and yellowed, but still somehow fresh-looking on this particular evening. She decides she will make sure it is empty every evening and begins drying the dishes. She looks at the clock. Five after seven. She wonders if she should have picked up Mama. She sets her towel on the counter and picks up the phone. She hesitates, then dials. Sally answers on the first ring.

"Sally? Has Mama left yet?"

"Zoe? That you, sweetheart?"

"Yeah. It's me."

"Your Mama ain't here, honey."

"How long ago did she leave? I was just wondering if I should have picked her up."

Zoe notes the pause.

"Your Mama hasn't been here at all today. She hasn't been in the shop for close to a month. Did she say she was coming in?"

Zoe stumbles, not fixing on Sally's voice anymore. "No. I mean, I think I misunderstood her. That's all. Thanks, Sally." She says good-bye and hangs up.

Not there? Where . . .

A familiar fear grips her, then explodes out of her.

"Mama?" she calls as she runs to the bathroom. *Damn!* She didn't check the bathroom. *"Mama!"* she calls again. She stops at the dark doorway, her hand whipping around to switch on the light. The curtain is drawn at the tub, and she jumps forward to tear it away. It's empty.

Only a white tub and nothing more.

Her knees are weak, and she holds on to the towel rack, closing her eyes, taking a breath, and another, feeling her heart beating against her throat.

She hears laughing, talking, good-byes, and then the front door opening. She loosens her grip on the rack and walks to the front room, just in time to see Mama closing the door behind her and then leaning back against it. She sees Mama's mouth moving but Zoe can't put the words together. It is a background jumble, as if she and Mama are moving on two different planes of time. As if her run to the bathroom has jolted her into another dimension. Has it? She feels nothing. She looks at Mama's eyes. They're unfocused, her pupils large, black, watery pools circled with a thin line of blue. Her dress is twisted and hanging off one shoulder, her dingy bra strap exposed. It tugs across her bloated middle, and Zoe sees the lines that have folded into her face since yesterday. Mama lifts her hand to brush her hair from her forehead, her beautiful forehead that Zoe has kissed so many times, but now its soft milkiness is a remembered dream. The planes she and Mama move on converge once again, and she hears Mama's words.

"What the hell you staring at?"

"Nothing, Mama," Zoe answers. "I'm staring at nothing."

Mama pushes past her, and Zoe hears her stumbling in her room, drawers slamming too loudly, closet doors swinging too wide. Mama returns in only her slip and settles on the couch with a half-filled glass in her hand. "Hand me the controls, will you, sugar?" There is no talk about Zoe's day, school, or her suspension. No questions.

She hands Mama the control and goes to her bedroom, not bothering to shut the door. She hears the click of the TV and chopped-up conversations as Mama flips through the channels. Chopped-up conversations that sound so familiar to her, like it is the only way people talk, talking but never finishing, finishing where there is no beginning.

She pulls the duffel from under her bed. She fills it. This time the decisions about what to put in seem easy. Her hands move methodically. She does the same with one pillowcase and then another. She hears Mama laugh and then soft whimpering, like an animal that has been wounded. Pauses, coughs, sobs, and the clink of the glass punctuate Mama's pleas.

"Sugar . . . ," she moans.

"Come here . . . ," she calls.

"I need to talk to you . . . ," she sobs.

Chopped-up conversations whose only beginning is Mama.

Zoe takes a piece of blue-lined paper from her notebook and begins writing. By the time she is finished and returns to the living room, Mama is asleep. She tapes the note to the TV screen.

> *There is Chinese in the refrigerator. The dishes are*
> *done. The utility bill is paid. I don't live here anymore.*
> *I live at 373 Lorelei Street.*
>
> > *I love you.*
> > *Zoe*

She loads the duffel and pillowcases into her car, and when she drives away, she leaves the chain-link gate swinging open wide.

TEN

Zoe paces the porch.

Walks in small circles.

Pulls in careful breaths.

Jiggles her hands to shake out trembling fingers.

It's 8:20, dark, much too late to be knocking on an old woman's door to take a room. She might scare the hell out of her if she rings the bell now. And after paying the electric bill today, she only has a hundred and thirty-six dollars left. Not even enough for a full month's rent. But tomorrow night she works, and she can usually count on her Thursday shift to bring in fifteen or sixteen in tips. She'll be extra nice to the customers. Her words will be all sugar—*Yes, ma'am* and *No problem, sir*—even if they ask for a thousand fucking substitutions. She'll squeeze twenty bucks out of tomorrow night. Will Opal wait until then?

The bulb to the right of the door glows a soft yellow, washing the gray-blue slats of the porch in a warm golden haze, blotting out the rest of Ruby, the world, in a safe circle of light that holds Zoe in. There is nowhere else to go. The room is already hers in her heart. She puts her finger to the bell, and with a jerky movement she forces it forward before she can change her mind. She hears a muted buzz, soft humming, and then the door swings open wide. Opal is smiling, her hair wrapped in a jeweled orange turban, a few stray curls spinning out near her ears, and a flowing purple caftan lapping near her ankles. She pushes open the screen door, waving Zoe in. "Ah, yes, yes," she warbles in her bird-like voice. "You made it. I was wondering when you'd get here."

Zoe steps inside. She tries to think back to her conversation with Opal. She is sure she never said anything about coming. "You knew I was coming?"

"Oh, not tonight. But I knew. I can read people's eyes. I read yours. They said today or tomorrow. Friday afternoon at the latest." Opal winks, and Zoe isn't sure if Opal is teasing or if she's a brick short of a load, but she likes the idea that someone could know what lives behind her eyes. She's not sure anyone has ever done that before. Opal guides her along by her elbow to a small table in the entryway, still humming her tuneless song. She opens its single shallow drawer and shuffles some papers aside. "Here we go." She places a small silver key in Zoe's palm, tweaks her head to the side, and says, "Welcome, Zoe Beth Buckman, to Opal's Lorelei Oasis." Opal looks up at the ceiling, squints her eyes, and then nods her head. "Yes. Yes. I like that. Though I did

58

consider Opal's Lorelei Hideout, too. Sounds dangerous and exciting. What do you think?"

"I—" Zoe is drawn to Opal's eyes. Can she read what lies behind them, too? For this moment, it seems she can. Wrinkled flesh gathers in folds around the old woman's eyes, circling the amber pools, the black pupils, the flecks of faded green, and Zoe sees . . . she is not sure she can put a name to it yet, but she recognizes it. It stirs up images . . . *searching beneath a pillow for a quarter that has replaced a tooth . . . sitting frozen for half an hour with a few bread crumbs in her cupped palm, barely breathing as a mourning dove steps closer and closer . . . driving home from Wal-Mart in the front seat of a jostling truck, stroking a brand new tennis racket laid across her lap* . . . a word something like *hope* . . . or maybe *possibility* is the better choice . . . possibility . . . the word she reads in Opal's eyes. "I like them both," she says.

Opal claps her hands and cackles. "Well, we'll stick with oasis—for today. Who knows about tomorrow!"

Yes, Zoe thinks. *Possibility is the word.* She reaches into her purse and takes out all her cash—one hundred and thirty-six dollars, most of it in bulky singles from her tips. Opal wrinkles up her nose and, still smiling, waves Zoe's fistful of money away.

"Oh, no, no. Let's not spoil our celebration by counting out that tonight. You can pay me tomorrow, and since we are already a week into September, let's make it an even hundred, shall we?" Before she has finished her last sentence, she is floating up the stairs, her caftan billowing behind her like a purple cloud, calling back to Zoe, "Might as well go in this way tonight. I'll show you where the bathroom is and then we can get your things. You did bring things, didn't you? Can't nest without your own things. Hurry, dear, the moon is almost up. You won't want to miss it! And you still have to meet the Count."

Zoe follows, suspecting that it may be more than a brick that Opal is missing, but she doesn't care. The room is finally in her grasp. The idea squeezes away her breath. *Is it really? And with money to spare? How can this be happening?* The room she thought could never be, the room that holds all her hopes, the room that holds possibility, is now steps away. Her lungs feel clamped and she gasps short, shallow breaths. *It's just the stairs,* she thinks, and she forces a deep, even breath.

The next ten minutes go by in a slow-motion dream. Zoe is watching from somewhere outside herself as she listens to instructions about jiggling the toilet handle, as she follows Opal to the room and is shown a closet with sheets and blankets, as she is introduced to Count Basil, an aging rottweiler who spends most of his time on the screened back porch. She continues to watch as if from a distant vantage point when she returns to her car and removes her duffel and returns again for the overflowing pillowcases. She listens and she watches like this is all happening to someone else.

As Opal leads her from one place to the next, Zoe takes in glimpses of the house. Its furnishings are eclectic, painting

Opal as a knitting grandmother in one corner and as a freak-ish collector in the next. A wine-colored overstuffed chair with delicate tatted arm coverings sits next to an ornately papered wall decorated with two curved, very lethal, four-foot sabers. Nearby, a life-size snarling grizzly carved from dark wood towers over a petite, doily-covered table holding a vase of fresh yellow snapdragons. It is a house of contra-dictions.

And finally the slow-motion lifetime that has passed in ten minutes is over, and Opal is saying good night, sweet dreams, don't forget the moon, and is shutting the door, and Zoe is alone. Alone, staring at her duffel on a bed, in a room, in a house, on a street named Lorelei. *Lorelei*. She runs her hand along the top of the duffel.

It is real.

She's here in a room that terrifies her but at the same time fills her with unspeakable lightness. Her hand passes over the duffel again; this time the zipper severing the silence. She takes her things from the bag and begins to nest, as Opal puts it. The picture of her and Kyle goes on the dresser, next to the ticking brass panther. Her clock radio is plugged in and set on the small table by the bed. Her jeans are placed in the dresser drawers, her other clothes hung in the large walk-in closet, her shoes placed neatly below them. Her jewelry box with the broken ballerina is set on the small half table by the front door. She pulls the heavy stone bulldog out from underneath the table to the middle of the room and faces it toward the door, on guard. In the dim light, it almost looks real. *It is my room,* she thinks, and the thought catches in her chest. *I can put it wherever I want. I don't have to worry about anyone tripping over it or calling it foolish, because it is my room.*

She closes her eyes, her throat constricts, and she swallows. She swipes her fingers across her wet lashes, and when she opens her eyes, she is caught by surprise. An unexpected laugh escapes her throat. She walks over to her bed and sits down on the edge, looking out her large-paned window at the moon Opal hurried her along for, mesmerized by the monstrous orange globe hanging just above the rooftops. It fills her window, like it is looking in, watching her, a smoky harvest moon there to welcome her to Opal's Lorelei Oasis.

It is only nine o'clock, and there are still things to put away, but instead she puts on her pajamas, brushes her teeth in the small kitchen sink, and crawls into bed. The springs creak softly under her weight, but it's not an unpleasant sound, more like satisfied sighs, and it hits her again that she is home. A home with a Count, an old lady, and a moon large and golden filling her window. The moon, she thinks, is probably looking in on Mama now, too. But Mama doesn't see. Not even if she is wide awake and gazing out the window. *What will happen to Mama?*

Zoe leans over to turn out the light, and when she lies back down in the darkness, she gasps. Hovering over her in the velvet sky are hundreds of stars. The faint spots on the indigo blue ceiling are transformed into hundreds of glowing stars.

The angels threw glitter up there just for you, Zoe. . . . Remember how special you are. . . .

But she knows it isn't true. If she were special, she would be home now, wrapped in Mama's arms, or room would be found at Clint and Patsy's. When you are really special, you are ranked first, not fourth on a team. And if you are truly special, people remember your name and know how to pronounce it.

She lets the thought roll into a place of numbness. A safe place she saves for it. It is a thought that has consumed her too many times, over and over again, until it is as old and lifeless as a joke that has been told too often. Something you can't laugh at—or cry at—anymore.

+ +
 +

Zoe stretches her legs across her bed and tucks her hands behind her head. A light breeze catches the gathered sheers at the edge of the window, making them billow out like a graceful, long-legged ghost. The breeze reaches her face, fresh and cool, carrying the scent of night jasmine. She breathes it in. She can't let herself care about worn-thin thoughts, because she has moved on. She is in a room of her own with a brass panther, a stone bulldog, a moon, stars, and an indigo sky full of possibility.

ELEVEN

Zoe slides into a middle seat in Mrs. Garrett's classroom.

A carefully chosen middle seat because it means nothing.

A back-row seat can say two things: *I am afraid of you* or, more often, *I hate you and this fucking class and I want to be the first one out of here*. A front-row seat can say two things: *I am not afraid of you* or, more often, *I want to be as close as I can to kiss your A-giving ass*. But the middle gives the teacher no fuel. Nothing to work with. That's what Zoe wants. To say nothing. If Mrs. Garrett wants a battle, she will have to drag Zoe out of the nothing-middle to get it. She has paid penance. She forged Mama's signature on the permission form for counseling and gave it to Mrs. Farantino. In return she got an admission slip back into class. Mrs. Garrett has already won. What more could she want?

Zoe is early. Her last class was just across the hall. She should have gone to the bathroom for a quick smoke, to smooth some of the tension out, but the first few days they are still watchful and teachers hover. She can't afford to get busted now. She remembers Mrs. Farantino's warning about good citizenship. It is four minutes until the bell rings, and the room is nearly empty, except for a few front-row types. Mrs. Garrett still hasn't made her appearance. One more period after this and Zoe can go home. Home. It is still such a strange new word. This morning when her alarm went off, she forgot for a few seconds where she was. She expected to hear Mama and the drone of a TV that was never turned off, or Mama opening a medicine cabinet searching for something to calm her stomach, or Mama shaking painkillers from a bottle for the cramping in her legs, or Mama and silence, the usual sound she heard.

Instead she heard the ruckus of bird chatter drifting through her open window. She crawled out of bed and looked out the window but couldn't see a single bird in the fig trees that lined the parkway. Still in her pajamas, she went to the outside landing of her stairs. She could see nothing except the edge of Opal's garden, but the sound was growing louder. She tiptoed down the stairs and walked to the backyard, her bare feet cold on the cement path. Turning the corner of the house, the deep backyard opened up to view and she saw the source of the commotion.

Opal, wearing a large straw hat tied to her head with a flowing green sash, was filling dish-shaped bird feeders hanging from trees. There had to be at least a dozen dishes. As Opal filled one and moved on to the next, the birds would flit back and forth, taking turns at the edge of the feeders and chirping their satisfaction. Zoe watched the look of exasperation and pride on Opal's wrinkled face as she warbled along with the birds, assuring them there was enough for all. She moved from one dish to the next with sweeping, dancing movements, confirming to Zoe that Opal didn't have her belt through all her loops.

But later, as Zoe walked downstairs to go to school and waved good-bye to Opal already working in her garden, she was stung by the clearness of Opal's eyes, and she knew Opal was anything but crazy.

+ * +

A whispered "You rule, woman" fills Zoe's ear, and she jumps back from Opal's Lorelei Oasis to Mrs. Garrett's classroom. Monica, the girl half of the Hernandez twins, is squeezing past and taking the seat next to her. She adjusts a tight black skirt across her chubby thighs and pulls her bra down through her shirt as she leans over like a seven-year-old with a big secret. "You've already become a classic. Everyone is spelling their names for their teachers. Don't bet on anyone doing it in here, though. Garrett would have killed anyone who so much as sneezed after you left."

Monica takes out a mirror and begins pulling at the hair piled on top of her head. Monica is efficient with her time, Zoe thinks—no moment wasted. Her brother, Jorge, is the same way. Fraternal or not, their minds think alike.

The classroom is nearly full now, and still no sign of

Mrs. Garrett. More students walk by and give Zoe approving pats on her back or shoulders. A few give her a thumbs-up sign. They are careful though, looking over their shoulders to be sure Mrs. Garrett hasn't come into the classroom yet. Zoe restrains a smile.

Another student she doesn't know comes in and faces her. She thinks he is going to acknowledge her, too, but instead says, "You're in my seat."

Zoe doesn't understand, but Monica snaps her mirror shut and quickly whispers, "I forgot to tell you! We have assigned seats now. I don't know where you're at."

Seniors never have assigned seats, Zoe thinks. She gathers her notebook and books and stands in the center aisle just as the bell rings and Mrs. Garrett enters the classroom. Standing alone, she feels like she's the center of a target and Mrs. Garrett is a poisonous dart heading her way. She freezes.

Mrs. Garrett walks past—slowly—her eyes briefly resting on Zoe. She speaks to the air as she passes, "When the bell rings, I expect *all* students to be in their seats." Zoe looks around. All students are in their seats—except her. She knows now, with certainty, that Mrs. Garrett has not moved on.

Zoe does not want to aggravate the situation. She wants to try. She says softly, in the most unaggressive voice she can muster, "I don't know where I sit."

Mrs. Garrett is now standing behind her lectern and

pointing to a poster on the wall. "Can you read a seating chart, Miss Buckman?"

So it's Miss Buckman now. She's never going to say my name—not correctly or any other way. Zoe takes a few steps forward so she can read the tiny lettering in each square. Everyone's names are listed first and last. Except hers. She is listed as Miss Buckman. The seat she is assigned to is in the first row, right beneath Mrs. Garrett's nose. Zoe looks over at Mrs. Garrett. Her gray eyes are unwavering and her jaw is set, the lines hard, intimidating, and full of knowing, just like Grandma's. Zoe's trying will not be enough for Mrs. Garrett. Not ever. She wishes now she hadn't forged Mama's name on that form, but there are still no other options for her.

Zoe hears every scuff of her shoes on the gritty linoleum as she steps forward and slides into the front and center seat, and she knows with every muffled cough and sideways glance from other students: Mrs. Garrett wants to throw her out of the classroom. There are no "sorry"s or counseling sessions in Mrs. Garrett's controlling, know-it-all world. But protocol must be followed. The rules. Forms have been signed. Now it is up to Zoe to blow it again. Mrs. Garrett probably thinks it will be easy. But Mrs. Garrett doesn't know her. Compared to the rest of Zoe's life, Mrs. Garrett is a cakewalk.

Zoe will wait her out.

The fifty-five-minute class moves along at an excruciatingly slow pace. Zoe raises her hand twice to offer answers.

Mrs. Garrett looks over her head and calls on other students. Zoe wonders why Mrs. Garrett put her front and center if she only plans to ignore her. *What is her fucking point?* The bell rings, and Zoe has not said a word the entire period. God, she needs a cigarette. But her next class is on the other side of campus and there really isn't time to sneak out to the parking lot. "C'mon," she says to Monica, tugging on her sleeve, "I need a lookout."

They slip into the bathroom at the end of the hall, and Zoe disappears into the last stall. Between the flushing toilets and the tinny sound of paper towel dispensers, Zoe listens for Monica's voice. She lights her cigarette and takes a deep drag, one that she pulls all the way down to her toes. She's only been smoking for a year, only half a pack a day—maybe a little more. She doesn't think she is addicted, physically, that is. It's more of a mental thing. Like polishing off a dozen Hershey's kisses when she is stiffed twice for tips in one night or eating a carton of pralines and cream when the guy who felt you up the night before is rubbing someone else's ass the next day. It is a gnawing that you have to satisfy, and cigarettes are a lot less fattening. Of course they'll turn your lungs to a tar pit—not good for tennis—but she only smokes half a pack. It isn't much. Just half a pack to get her through the day. And she has a lot of days she needs getting through.

She takes another deep drag and hears Monica blurt out in song, "L is for the way you LOOK at me!" The signal. She drops her cigarette in the toilet, flushes, and waves her hand to clear the air. Monica sings on. "O is for the only one I SEE!" Her voice echoes in the concrete cavern like she is auditioning for a musical. Zoe has the feeling that Monica enjoys the role of lookout. She steps out before Monica can go on to the next line. A faint haze of smoke follows her. She looks across the bathroom and decides she can finish the next line herself—V is for VERY bad timing.

Mrs. Garrett is staring at her again, looking down her nose, her head tilted slightly to the side, like she is looking at a useless bug. Zoe looks away and continues the bathroom act, swishing her hands under the faucet and reaching for a paper towel. Her mind races under the silent stare. *Shit. She can't prove anything. It's only a damn cigarette. What's her problem?* Zoe throws her towel away, and she and Monica walk out without a word from Mrs. Garrett, but Zoe still feels the heaviness of the stare and wonders how a simple look could make her feel like so much less than everyone else.

TWELVE

"You don't have to wait. Go on."

Zoe adjusts her butt on the edge of the curb and stretches her legs out. She doesn't want to wait. She wants to go home. To her new home. School let out fifteen minutes ago, and the parking lot is clear. But she says what Carly wants to hear, what she needs to hear. "I don't mind. It gives us a chance to talk." They have already talked about the unfairness of speeding tickets on perfectly flat stretches of highway, Carly's lack of wheels, Zoe's suspension and the wave of careful pronunciations infiltrating all the classrooms, and finally, Zoe's forthcoming counseling.

Carly looks at her watch. "Reid said his stupid meeting would only last five minutes. Just long enough to find out a couple things about their first play." She shakes her head. "He's probably already auditioning for every damn part."

Zoe smiles. Carly knows her brother too well. Reid lives for drama—in and out of the theater. This past summer he got the starring role in *Little Shop of Horrors* at the community playhouse. And for drama out of the theater, he got to spend the night in jail for chaining himself to an old eucalyptus on the corner of Algheny and First. The tree had to go to widen the road, but Reid didn't see it that way. "A tree has rights, too," he said. "It's been here longer than us and is way better-looking than the mayor." The city didn't agree, and neither did his parents. Besides a night in a cell, that drama also cost him a long-planned fishing trip to the Gulf with his dad. Carly went instead and loved every minute.

Zoe doesn't understand what could have excited Carly so much about a fishing trip. The idea of bobbing on a boat for the sole purpose of pulling bloody-lipped fish out of the sea doesn't appeal to her at all. She and Carly are different in a lot of ways, most ways probably. She isn't even sure you could call them best friends. What does "best" mean? she wonders. But they are loyal friends, longtime friends for sure, ever since seventh grade when they were both alone at lunch at a new junior high and they latched on to each other to save the humiliation of being alone.

Zoe had had friends in elementary school, but one had moved away over the summer, and the other had switched to Saint Pat's Catholic School. Carly had been her life raft. Standing alone on an asphalt sea at a junior high is just as deadly as being adrift in a real one when you are a girl who doesn't wear the right shoes and your mother hasn't thought to get you a bra for your emerging nipples. Of course Carly did have the right shoes, and her breasts were already full and well-covered, but her teeth hadn't been fixed yet, and she mumbled through a hand that always hovered just below her nose. Her braces have been off for a couple of years now, her smile straight and beautiful, but Zoe notices that when Carly is nervous, her hand still shoots up, on guard at her upper lip, braced for taunts that still have life in secret memories. Zoe guesses some scars are etched on the skin, some in the brain, the ones in the brain much deeper and lasting.

She hasn't told Carly about moving. She wonders if she should. It might make Carly feel guilty, like she should have known, like she should have offered her place, like she shouldn't have a mother who is so different from Zoe's, like she shouldn't have a father who is still alive and takes her on fishing trips. But more than worrying about Carly's guilt, Zoe feels the room on Lorelei is still part of a dream world— thin and gauzy and fragile. Like it could swirl away into the air at any moment. Her urge to leave is stronger. She has to hurry. Has to anchor it down by being there. She stands.

"How about if I just give you a ride?"

"Nope. Part of the punishment, too." Carly rolls her big brown eyes. "Lack of wheels is only effective if it inconveniences you. Mom says no rides with friends—only Reid." She stands with Zoe and swats at her butt to brush off dust. "She'll get over it fast enough, though. She doesn't realize how much she relies on me to run errands. No way is she going to send Reid to the store for tampons. I know

73

something will come up that will have me behind the wheel by this weekend." Carly smooths a damp strand of her short, curly brown hair from her forehead. "Go ahead. He'll be here soon."

"You sure?" Zoe knows Carly hates to be alone. Brain scars, she thinks.

Carly's brows pull together, and she blows a puff of air out between her lips like being alone is nothing to her. "Go," she says.

And Zoe does.

THIRTEEN

It is eight minutes from the school parking lot to the shaded parkway. Eight minutes for every worry to crowd her mind. *What if? What if? What if Mama needs me, what if Kyle calls, what if Opal changes her mind, what if Mama . . . Mama . . . Mama?* It always starts and ends with Mama. The what ifs are only blotted out when Zoe's feet stamp out a frenzied rhythm up the stairs and she slides her key into the lock, throws open the door, and it is all still there. The bed. The jukebox. The stone bulldog on guard. The air. Hers.

Every corner is still there.

She walks to the bed and lies facedown, her arms spread wide, her fingers digging into the fabric, holding to be sure, tossing on a crest between laughter and tears, and then she lifts her head, focuses, and the gauzy dream is solid. Her breathing slows, and she takes in the comfort of the room. She lets it fill her, settle her like ballast in a boat. And then, when the calm has coursed to her fingertips, she gets up and begins taking a few last items from a pillowcase propped in the corner. The need to finish her nesting is obvious. Of course. Down to her marrow she needs this. She pushes thoughts of Mama aside and finishes finding order for the years of jumble she brought from home.

A tuneless hum tumbles from her throat and floats on the air as she works. She carefully places a small, rose-flowered photo album at the end of the window seat on a tasseled tangerine pillow. She fluffs the other pillows lining the seat and then rearranges them. Their bright mismatched colors remind her of a worn but loved box of crayons. Next, she sets a tiny wooden tray on the dresser next to the picture of her and Kyle and places half a dozen perfumes on it. She sprays a blast of Summer Morning into the air and inhales. She marvels. She controls the smell of her room, too. She sprays another blast and sets the bottle with the others. Her battered stuffed Eeyore is placed between the two pillows on her bed. His matted gray-blue fur looks nice, she thinks, against the tiny winding-leaf pattern of the spread. Opal said she had another spread if Zoe preferred, but the delicate leafy design is perfect for under the star-filled ceiling. It will stay.

She continues to empty her pillowcase until it is flat and then she neatly folds it and sets it on a shelf in her closet. Her closet. *It's done,* she thinks, and there are still two hours before her shift starts at the diner. Enough time to smell the Summer Morning or rearrange everything all over again if she chooses. Or maybe time to run to the store for a few things to fill the refrigerator.

A refrigerator. She has a refrigerator to fill. Her *own* refrigerator.

After paying Opal and buying lunch and half a tank of gas, she still has twenty-two dollars. Today that sounds like a fortune. More than she needs for a few things. The room is working. It's working.

She walks out of the deep closet to the stone dog and smiles. "You're doing a good job," she says, and hunches over to move him a few inches to the right— But then she is raising, lifting . . . going from crouched and hovering over the dog to straightening her legs . . . pulling back her shoulders . . . lifting her chin . . . uncurling her spine . . . every movement noted and frozen in time by a sharp knock at the door.

She instinctively knows. It is not Opal. But who? No one knows she is here.

Except Mama.

The knock comes again, hard, demanding attention.

But Mama's knock would not be so forceful. It would be slurred, undecided, barely there. Barely interested.

It is not Mama.

The knock comes again. Impatient.

She walks to the door, forcing a smile, ready to say hello, ready to see how it feels to answer *her* door. She turns the knob and swings the door wide.

Gray eyes pierce her own, and a hand lifts up, casting a flapping shadow like a bird across her face. The hand comes back down before she can twist away, and the black shadow becomes a white explosion across Zoe's ear and eye. She winces and presses the side of her head but keeps her eyes on the gray ones holding her own.

"What the hell do you think you're doing?"

"Grandma—"

"Don't say a word, missy! You hear me? You just listen!"

"But, Gra—"

"You leave a note? You leave a note taped to the TV?" Her words come out strained, like tight cords ready to snap. "You know what that did to your mama? What she's been doing all day long? Crying! You hear that? Crying! Crying her eyes out for a hard, ungrateful daughter!"

Zoe stares hard at Grandma. She wants Grandma to look into her face. *I'm not invisible. Just look. That's all.*

But instead Zoe sees the saliva gathering at the corners of Grandma's mouth, working up into silvery threads that slide into the creases of her mouth because Grandma will not swallow, will not take the time to lick the corners with her tongue, because she has too much to say and no time at all to search Zoe's face.

"Your mama's had enough heartache without you adding to it! Who do you think—"

"Grandma!" Zoe hardly recognizes her own voice. It is loud and desperate and stops the wrinkled lips midsentence. "Grandma," she says again, but she can't go farther. Zoe looks away, examining the doorjamb, picking at the

creamy paint with her fingernail, afraid, as the words finally run out of her mouth to a place where she can never take them back. "I can't. I can't watch anymore." But they are still not the words she wanted. Her brain has sidestepped.

Grandma's head tilts to the side, her voice lowers and each word comes out distinctly separate like she is afraid, too. "Can't watch what?"

"I can't watch Mama . . . die."

"What?" Fear explodes in Grandma's eyes at the suggestion of losing her favorite child. Her upper lip lifts and freezes unnaturally, exposing yellowed teeth anchored in receding gums. "What are you saying?"

"Mama's dying, Grandma. It's the alcohol. Mama's . . . an alcoholic." There. She said it. It's done. And it doesn't sound silly or impossible. It sounds true.

Grandma shakes her head and sighs. Her voice softens. "Beth, Beth." Zoe listens carefully to her middle name said softly, almost tenderly. Grandma reaches out and momentarily cups Zoe's chin. "Now, Beth, that's a fool notion you've gotten hold of—probably in one of your classes at school. A few drinks don't make someone an alcoholic."

"But, Grandma—"

"Now you hear me out. I ain't denying your mama tips it a little often, but she's going through a hard time right now. That's all. Just a hard time. What with your daddy—" Grandma raises her eyebrows and sighs again. "Well, with him passing on—especially the way it happened—well, like

I said, she's just going through a hard time. This'll pass. But in the meantime she needs her family to be sticking close by her."

As Grandma continues to speak she opens her purse and shakes out a cigarette from a nearly empty pack. She lights it, pulls hard, and blows smoke out through one side of her sagging mouth. "You don't get over something like this overnight, and your daddy, well, he was the love of your mama's life, so that's—"

"*Love of her life?* She threw him *out,* Grandma. That's why he was at the motel in the first place."

Grandma smirks, and smoke drifts out her nose. "I know how it looks, but that was nothing. Lovers have quarrels all the time. It wasn't their first, and no one guessed it would be their last, but that doesn't change how she felt about him. She was crazy about that man," and then under her breath as she always had to do when talking about Daddy, she added, "though only the Lord knows why."

Zoe feels the wound of Grandma's familiar comment fresh each time. She is half of Daddy. Half of Daddy stands before Grandma right now. His dark eyes, dark hair, and maybe more. But there is no sense, Zoe thinks, in digging open old wounds, when fresh ones lie before them. And Grandma has to at least hold to the logic of time. "But, Grandma, it's been almost two years since Daddy died, and even long before that Mama and Daddy were drinking—"

"You just trust your granny. You hear?" She places her

hands on Zoe's shoulders and holds her squarely. Zoe doesn't move. She wants to believe. She wants to trust. She wants to hear what Grandma can say that will change it all and make Zoe wrong. She waits.

"I've been around a lot longer than you," Grandma says, "and so has your mama. And right now she needs you. That's all you need to worry about." Grandma steps back and takes another puff of her cigarette. "Now let's push all this nonsense aside. I'll help you get your things together and then follow you back home to smooth things out with your mama. I'll do that for you. I'll make things right between you two again, you hear?"

"Yes, Grandma," Zoe whispers.

But she wonders what Grandma has just said. She tries to grab hold of the wispy threads that said nothing, but maybe everything. How will Grandma make things right? Did she say? Where are the answers Zoe thought she would get? Is she wrong about Mama being an alcoholic? What is the nonsense? Everything that Zoe has been afraid of for so long? Or all the possibility she hoped for? Or everything about Zoe? Did Grandma ever really look into her eyes, or did she just see Daddy's black pupils that don't account for any time or thought at all?

Grandma reaches out to push Zoe aside to enter the room. Zoe's room.

Zoe shifts to block her. "You can't come in, Grandma!"

Grandma stiffens.

"It's the landlord," Zoe explains. "She doesn't allow smoking. That's all. Besides, it will just take me a few minutes . . . to get my stuff together. Why don't you go finish your smoke in your car and I'll be right down."

Grandma takes another puff. "All right," she says, measuring her words. Zoe knows she is happy to finish her cigarette, unhappy about taking orders. The nicotine wins the draw. "But hurry, I've got other things to do today."

I do, too, Grandma. I have to go to work in two hours. Did you know that? But the words stay hidden in her head, crowding for room among all the other unsaid words. She watches Grandma return to her car to wait, her steps heavy on the stairs, heavy on Zoe's brain.

Zoe waits until Grandma disappears around the corner of the garage, then retreats to her room. She bends down, slides her empty duffel from beneath her bed but then stands again staring at it, not sure what to put in first. She sits down on the edge of the bed, stroking the tall carved bedpost. *Put something in, Zoe. Something.*

But she can't think what that first something should be.

She stares at the frayed straps of the duffel and thinks, *It is over.* The room is over. She was wrong. She made Mama cry. She is an ungrateful, terrible daughter. Grandma said so. And if those aren't reasons enough to be packing her bags, she knows Grandma has a steady supply of more to take their place. She always does. All this waiting and yelling and crying for Mama.

Why?

Why always Mama?

She lets one thought tumble into another, pushing the packing away. *Push, Zoe. Think.* She wonders, if she were Uncle Clint's daughter, would Grandma have come barging her way in? Would it have been worth her bother? Zoe thinks not. Mama is Grandma's favorite. It has always been clear that she is, but *why?*

Zoe flips through the pages of Uncle Clint's life like she is searching a book for answers. Something that would explain why she must now pack her duffel and leave her room. Why Mama and not Uncle Clint? He's a nice enough man. Always clean-shaven. His hair thinning a little on top, but always neatly trimmed and combed. He has a steady job. Nothing fancy, just throwing mail at the Cooper Springs Annex, but it's reliable. Why shouldn't he be the favorite? Would she still have the room if he was? He treats Aunt Patsy respectfully and keeps his yard weeded and green and plants a vegetable garden every spring. He's not the life of the party, that's for sure, usually busying himself with chores like hauling soda from the garage, or adding ice to the cooler, or emptying the trash, or hanging out on the driveway and fiddling underneath someone's hood since he's handy with tools. He's quiet, dull even, but you can count on him. Counting on someone is worth a lot. Shouldn't that make him a favorite? Aunt Patsy calls him the salt of the earth, which Zoe takes to mean he is one of the plainer spices, but maybe the most important. But not to Grandma. She always has a cutting remark about him. If he'd gone to college, he wouldn't be stuck in a government job. If he was thriftier, he'd have a real home instead of a trailer. If he put his foot down once in a while, he wouldn't have a houseful of hooligans running through it all the time.

His trailer is a double-wide manufactured home on an acre of land, and the hooligans are the abundant eleven-year-old friends of her cousin, Wain. Grandma always sees the glass half empty instead of half full when it comes to Uncle Clint. *Why?* And Aunt Nadine, the oldest of Grandma's kids, well, Zoe doesn't know a lot about her, but she knows she's not a favorite, either. She's the mysterious aunt no one talks much about, or at least they're not supposed to. She moved away to Brownsville when Zoe was four. Brownsville is about as far as you can get from Ruby and still be in Texas. Aunt Nadine only comes back once every several years, for a holiday, a wedding, or maybe a funeral. She came to Daddy's funeral, and that was the last time Zoe saw her. She popped in and out in two days and stayed at a motel, which started a commotion with Grandma, but then Aunt Nadine was gone again just as fast, so the fight had no fuel. Aunt Nadine seemed to have a wall around herself as far as Grandma was concerned. Grandma didn't have many cutting remarks for Aunt Nadine. Mostly no remarks at all.

But when Grandma talked about *Mama,* a change came over her. Zoe noticed her stature actually seemed to change, like she was growing bigger and stronger, and her gray, empty eyes sprang to life. *What made that happen?* Mama is the youngest, her baby, is that it? She has heard Grandma call Mama her miracle baby. Grandma said her female parts were scarred and torn, and the doctors with their high-falutin' degrees said there would be no more babies. And then Mama came along and proved them all wrong. . . . Or maybe it was Grandma who did the proving? Was that it? Grandma had to keep on proving that they were wrong and everything about Mama was right?

Or maybe it has nothing to do with being a miracle baby at all but that Mama is so needy and Clint and Nadine aren't? Mama *is* needy. Maybe that's what it's all about. A child who still needs Grandma, or maybe a child Grandma is still holding out hope for. Like a baby bird that has fallen out of the nest and the mother abandons the rest to save the one. Is that it? Is that why she is losing the room? Why she has to go back? Because Mama is a lost bird?

But it's probably none of those things, and Zoe knows she can't ask. Some things are not meant to be brought up—like Daddy patting Mama's tummy and begging her not to get rid of the baby inside. Some things might gnaw inside of you, like the awful way Daddy died, and other things might squeeze your heart so you can't take a breath, like watching Mama's legs starve away. But some things. *Some things.* They don't have a real life if they aren't put to words, and it is probably best just to pack your bags and not rock the boat because if you do, you just might knock the boat clean over and make everybody drown, including yourself.

Drowning.

How painful is it? Zoe wonders.

"Beth! What are you doing? You haven't packed a thing! You think I have all day to—"

Zoe springs from the edge of the bed. "I'm not going, Grandma."

"What?"

The words jumped from her throat, and she's surprised at them, too. "I'm not going back." She pauses and then steps closer to Grandma. The surprise is over, and she adds more deliberately, "I'm *never* going back."

Grandma fills the doorway, the afternoon sun squeezing past her silhouette in hot lines of light. "I heard the not going back part, but I want some explaining to go with it!"

The words are there. Ready. Rehearsed a hundred times over on dark, tear-filled nights, but they are held back by fears that opening up one secret could make them all come pouring out—even ones she doesn't want to know—fears that whisper in her ear, *Be silent. Be careful.*

"Well, *Beth*?"

"I'm just not going," Zoe answers softly.

"And that's what I'm supposed to tell your mama? You just *aren't*?" Grandma tilts her head and looks down her nose at Zoe. It's a look that makes Zoe want to curl inside of herself so the whole world is black. It's a look she has seen so many times before.

"You don't have to tell her anything at all," Zoe says. "She knows where I live if she wants to hear it from me."

Grandma knows Mama will never show up and so she changes the direction of the conversation. Zoe has always noticed that about her—her skill at maneuvering conversations and lives.

"What about the car?" she asks. "You think you're gonna keep that thing?" Her voice lowers, and she spits the words out like well-aimed bullets. "Think again, missy."

Zoe hadn't thought about the car. No one has keys to it but her—she made sure of that the last time Mama was arrested. She has all the keys for safekeeping. The only way Grandma is going to be able to take it away is to have it towed, and Zoe wouldn't put that past her. "When Mama can drive again, I'll give it back."

Grandma moves on, searching for the next soft spot. "You think you're going to make it on your own? You're only seventeen! You sling hash, for God's sake! You think you can make it on *that*?" The look again. She fumbles in her purse for another cigarette and lights it as she continues to talk. The cigarette is tucked in her knobby fingers like a glowing pointer that she shakes at Zoe. "You ain't gonna make it. You hear me, Beth? You'll be back. You'll come crawling back for forgiveness, and you know what? We'll give it to you, too. Your mama and me. Because we're family, and that's what family does. You'll come begging and crying, and we'll take you back. But things'll be *different,* that's for sure. You can count on that. You hear me, Beth? You hear what I'm saying?"

"I hear," Zoe says.

Grandma shakes her head and narrows her eyes to puckered slits. She leans so close Zoe can smell her smoky breath. "Family sticks together—real family, that is. But I think you got all of your daddy's blood and none of your mama's. I guess you're hardly family at all." She shakes her head one last time and leaves.

Zoe walks to the landing, watching Grandma plod down the steps. When she gets to the bottom of the stairs, she turns and calls, "And don't bother coming to Kyle's party on Saturday. Only family's invited. Unless, that is, you've already come crawling back by then."

She watches Grandma disappear around the corner of the garage, and with crushing clarity Zoe knows that she will die—she will truly die—before she ever crawls back. She forces a breath, and another wave of knowing hits her. Nothing will keep her from Kyle's party on Saturday. Kyle is more hers than anyone's.

She goes back in and closes the door, the door to her room on Lorelei Street, and in that instant, with the clicking of the latch, Ruby is no longer small. It is a large town of close-knit families, best friends arm-in-arm, houses with well-kept gardens and easy laughter, conversations buzzing over phone lines, and life of which Zoe is not a part. Ruby is suddenly very, very large, and Zoe is very, very small. She is only seventeen, and she only slings hash, and if she were to slip away into inky black nothingness, would anyone really notice?

FOURTEEN

Opal hugs a bag of groceries with one arm and lifts the other arm to Zoe. She waves her twiggy fingers, and Zoe thinks her smile is too young for her wrinkled apple face. It reminds her of Kyle, smiling from somewhere down deep, as much for himself as anyone else. Zoe waves back. She manages a smile, too. She knows her smile doesn't come as freely or as deeply, but it is the best she can do, and Opal nods her head like she is so pleased that Zoe saw her.

She puts the car into drive. Soon Opal is out of her vision and she only sees the dappled flash of light on her hood as she races down Lorelei Street to work. She is only at Carmichael when another flash comes into view. The red warning light glows on the instrument panel. She needs oil. *Shit.* Why now? She thinks she can make it to the gas station half a block from Murray's. Didn't she just add oil? How long can you drive with the oil light on? She doesn't know. Grandma would just love to see this. Would love to see her burning up Mama's engine. But it's only oil. It's only a couple of bucks. She'll take care of it better than Mama would have.

With each block she feels the glowing red light twisting something inside of her tighter. *Ungrateful. Am I really?* The light seems to grow brighter. *The engine and I may poof at the same time,* she thinks. *Poof. No more engine. No more Zoe. No more nothing. Would that be so bad?*

Six blocks later she turns off into Thrifty Gas and Garage. She rolls down the window and asks the attendant for oil. "I'm in a hurry, if you don't mind. I'm on my way to work." He obliges and lifts her hood. He pulls out the stick, shakes his head, wipes it with a blue paper towel, and shoves it in again. He shakes his head again when he pulls it out, and Zoe's fingers tighten on the steering wheel. Maybe she drove it too far. Maybe the engine is ruined already. God, she can never face Grandma with that.

The attendant walks over to her window, carefully holding the stick like there is a virus on the end. "I can add more oil if you want, but I'd just be adding it to sludge. When was the last time you changed the oil in this thing?"

Changed the oil? She has never changed the oil. "I think it's been a while," she says. "Does it need it?"

He silently nods his grease-smudged face like the condition is too grave to utter a word.

"How much?" she asks.

"Change the oil, new filter, and top off your other fluids for twenty-nine bucks. Best thing you can do for your car.

Simple stuff like that'll keep it running for years. Could have it done in half an hour."

Zoe sighs. She doesn't have half an hour. She doesn't have twenty-nine bucks. But she needs a car that will last for years. A car that Grandma can't blame her for trashing. "Can I leave it and pick it up around nine?"

"Sure thing."

She grabs her purse and gets out of the car, dropping the keys into the attendant's greasy palm. She is afraid to ask but she does. "And can I pay when I pick it up?"

"You bet."

So much for groceries for the refrigerator. She heads for Murray's, grateful that she didn't burn up the engine. Mama would have. It is still light outside, but she can see Murray's neon sign half a block away already glowing with its red and yellow lights.

Ungrateful? What did Grandma mean by that? Zoe grabs a cigarette from her purse for one last smoke before her shift begins. She notices the pack is nearly empty. Didn't she just open it this morning? It must have been yesterday. *What should I be grateful for?* She lights up and takes a drag, wondering if she looks like Grandma when she does. She tries to keep her face smooth and light as she inhales, her chin drawn up and her eyes soft and round.

Grateful? For what? That Mama didn't get rid of her when she was nothing more than a peanut inside of her? Grateful for all of Kyle's crappy diapers? Grateful for all the times

Mama didn't show up for parent conferences at school? She almost smiles—maybe she should be grateful for that. Or maybe grateful for all the life-sucking, meandering, tearful monologues that squeeze the spirit right from her heart and have everything to do with Mama and nothing, nothing to do with Zoe? *I'm only seventeen, Grandma. Don't I deserve a life, too?*

The streets of Ruby are busy, and the sound of her footsteps is lost in the rumble of the trucks and cars whizzing past her. Everyone is in a hurry to get home. Home. So they can enjoy the twilight, the brief rosy wash of quiet before evening brings its own busyness. She slows her pace and searches for that feeling, a fluttering hint she remembers, so she must have known it once. You can't remember if it never happened.

There are things . . .

She is grateful . . . grateful. . . . Mama holding her, wiping tears and hair from her cheeks when she has her first period on the bus and Kenny Beeson announces it to everyone. Mama whispering and cooing over and over again that she is a woman now and Kenny is nothing but a jerk-off little boy. Grateful. Mama, bragging on the phone to Aunt Nadine that Zoe is five-six and still growing, Zoe with silky black hair, Zoe with eyes that can stop traffic. Mama said those things. Grateful. Mama, leaning over, so slowly, tenderly, kissing Daddy's cold lips when Zoe couldn't even walk up to the coffin. Mama. Beautiful Mama.

Grateful.

FIFTEEN

"Easy on the mayo!" Zoe reminds the cook. It's on the ticket, but if he forgets, she is the one who will pay the price, and tonight more than ever she needs the tips. Her voice is cheerful. She cannot sound like a nag, either, or her pleas will backfire. She walks a tightrope as thin as spaghetti as she turns, smiles to the sleazebag at the counter who cannot keep his eyes off her off-limits breasts, and asks, "More coffee?"

"If you're offerin'," he says, "I'm takin'." His voice suggests everything his eyes ask for.

Zoe pours. She knows where she would like to pour it, but that would probably nix her tip. Maybe. She moves on to table seven, three elderly women who are finishing up soup, rolls, and water. Not a high tab, but Zoe knows how they tip anyway. Fifty cents from each of them, no matter what they order. It's the same routine every Thursday night after their Bible meeting. She pours them more water and lays their bill on the table. At table six she refills a young couple's iced teas and lets them know their Island burgers will be right up. She smiles, maybe even from somewhere deep, at least as deep as a beef patty can take you. Island burgers in the middle of Ruby. A few months ago it was Fiesta dogs. That one didn't last. You had to love Murray.

Her tables have been light tonight, but she can't complain. Charisse and Deirdre have had even fewer tables. Zoe has kept count. Every time Murray seats someone she notices. She has to. The counter is seat yourself, though, divided half and half between Charisse and Zoe. At dinnertime most folks want to sit at a table, so it is not too busy. Only the sleazebag on Zoe's half and another customer occupy it now. Zoe wishes she had the other customer. She glances at him when she can, notices his worn blue jeans and his clean white T-shirt that fits him way too nicely, but his attention is held by a thick book open on the counter beside him. She guesses he must be twenty or so, maybe Hispanic. His hair is dark, and his arms are the same rich color of the toasted almonds she nibbles from the top of Murray's coffee cake. He alternately scoops forkfuls of mashed potatoes and chicken-fried steak. She wonders what could be so damn interesting in his book that he can't be friendly, and then she wonders why the hell she cares.

She returns to the sleazebag and, though she hates to ask, she knows she must before she can lay down the bill. "Anything else I can get for you tonight?" Her voice is pitch-perfect, her smile sterling, and she knows if Reid were watching he would applaud her. She has never worked so hard in her life.

The sleazebag shifts in his seat. He grins. She can tell he is so pleased with the setup. She supposes she shouldn't give him another thought. He probably has the teeniest, weeniest penis, and this is his way of making up for it. *We all have ways of compensating,* she thinks.

"What else have you got for me, honey?"

She scrutinizes his oily face. He has to be twice her age, somewhere in his thirties at least. His hair is thin and stiff, sprayed in place so his scalp won't be revealed by an unexpected breeze. He holds his hands oddly, like he doesn't know what to do with them. They are large and meaty and awkward and don't match his thin, angled body. *What else have I got for you?*

"Just what's on the menu," she says.

He leans forward and lowers his voice. "Is that all? I thought maybe you had some special desserts you wanted to tell me about." He says "special" like he has invented the word. Like he is a come-on genius and she will melt.

It must be so small, Zoe thinks. *No bigger than a gherkin.*

"No," she says. "Just what's on the menu." She stays cheerful, happy. Oscar-worthy. Reid would be proud. Oil changes take priority over humiliating dirtbags.

"Then I think I'll pass. Maybe next time."

"Sure. Next time," she says, and she slides the bill across

to him. "Have a good evening." She hurries away to deliver the Island burgers to the young couple before he can say anything else.

After she has delivered the burgers and gathered her dollar-fifty tip from table seven, she catches Murray at the cash register. "Hey, Mur, any chance of me picking up a shift on Saturday night? I could really use the money."

The squint of his eyes and the tilt of his head answer her question, but he goes ahead and explains anyway. "Pretty top-heavy already, Zoe, and you've seen how it is tonight—Saturdays haven't been much better. Between the new Buffet Basket in Cooper Springs and the grand opening of the Rocket Gourmet in Duborn, I'm getting squeezed from both ends like a rat in a snake's belly."

"You're no rat, Mur," she says. "Things will get better. No one has chicken-fried steak like you. You're a landmark in Ruby." She's sorry she asked. She already knew things were tight, and now she has rubbed it in deeper with Murray. He added Tammy Barton to the payroll last month when her scum-licking husband ran out on her and their two kids. Tammy can't balance two plates on her arm to save her life, but Murray knew she was desperate. There aren't a lot of jobs in Ruby. Most folks commute to Abilene or even farther. Zoe knows she is lucky to have this job—especially with a boss like Murray.

"But if someone calls in sick, I'll be sure and call you first."

And then, like he has arrived at a better solution, he adds, "Or maybe we could let a few rats loose at Buffet Basket—that might send more customers this way."

Zoe forces a smile, struggling to keep up her Oscar performance but only thinking how broke she is, how alone, and how there is no one to help. It seeps into her, weighing her down like a sinking boat. She lifts her voice, for Murray's sake and maybe for her own, too. "That's what I like about you, Mur. Always thinking. Island burgers one day, rats the next."

Three customers walk in the door, and Murray whispers to Zoe, "Ix-nay the at-ray talk. We don't want to send 'em the other direction." He grabs three menus and welcomes them, leading them to a booth. At the same time, the sleazebag arrives at the cash register and Murray asks Zoe to ring him up.

"Sure," she says, noting her poor timing. Seeping. Sinking. But why should anything go well for her today?

He fans a fat wad of bills, pulls out a twenty, and hands it to her along with his tab. She notices his hands again, thick, heavy, and clumsy, resting like two hams on the counter. "So, things are a little tight, huh?" he says.

"Good hearing," Zoe answers.

"I'm good at lots of things," he says.

Zoe glances back to where he was sitting. The tip is already there. Nothing to lose.

"Well, you're a good talker, anyway."

She hands him his change and he fans the bills once again, inserting his change in between. He shoves the wallet in his hip pocket and smiles, his ham-hock hands dangling at his sides. "You have a good evening now, you hear?" he says and leaves.

Zoe heads straight to his seat to retrieve her tip. Five dollars? It is three times what he should have left. Grandma's accusation fills her head. Ungrateful. *Is she?* Was he just trying to be friendly? Did the poor perv just want to be noticed? Was that too much to ask? Just to be noticed? The way she wants the guy at the end of the counter to notice her? Isn't that all anyone really wants—someone's eyes to look into you instead of through you?

She watches Charisse fill the book guy's water glass. He lifts his gaze from his book, smiles, and thanks her. Charisse is married with three kids. *She can never appreciate that smile like I can,* Zoe thinks. But life is never fair, never even, never sensible. Look at Mama and Daddy. They fought like cats and dogs, but Grandma says Daddy was the love of Mama's life. If love is a lot of fighting and pain, then maybe life does make sense after all.

She runs her hands through the tips in her pocket. She knows to the penny how much money is there. Exactly $13.75. Her groveling, jumping, and smiles didn't get her far, and now her shift is over. *Never even, never fair.* After she tips the cook and pays the garage, she will have $5.25 to last her until Sunday when she works again.

Mama probably drinks away that much in a day, she thinks.

She wraps two biscuits in a napkin and fills a paper cup with orange juice before she leaves. She will put those in her refrigerator. Her refrigerator. *I am grateful. I am.*

She takes a last look at the guy at the end of the counter. He is studying his book again, his fingers running down the page. She wishes she was half as interesting as his book. She clocks out and leaves, walking through Murray's parking lot past the grimy oil pump she usually parks next to. Like the others that sprinkle the Ruby community in odd, unexpected places, it has a matching grimy chain-link fence around it. It groans its usual greeting. A groan that always seems to be pleading, always sad. She offers her usual greeting in return.

"Someday," she whispers. "Someday."

SIXTEEN

She takes a detour.

It's for the coffee can, she thinks. For the thousand pennies that must be in the coffee can. It's hers after all. Just a quick detour to get what is hers.

The gate still swings open. Light glows through yellowed shades.

She pushes the door open. "Mama?" she whispers, so softly it hardly creases the air.

There is no answer. She didn't expect there would be. She goes to her closet and quietly slides the door open. The old coffee can, heavy with pennies, grates and chinks as she slides it from her shelf. She tucks it into the nook of one arm and slides the closet shut with the other. Mama will never know she was here. Her breath barely rises in her chest as she walks down the hallway, but then she stops.

Why, Zoe? Why don't you just leave? Run?

But something pulls inside of her. It feels like Daddy, whispering in her ear, *Just keep an eye on Kyle for a few minutes, a few minutes, I'll be back, keep him safe for me, that's a good girl, my good little Zoe.*

She closes her eyes, but it doesn't make the pulling go away. She wants to throw the coffee can against the wall and hear a thousand clattering pennies shatter the silence, a thousand tinny voices falling to the floor, spinning, rolling out of control, anything but Daddy's whispers.

She hugs the can closer and reaches for Mama's doorknob. A quick look. That's all. Just to be sure. She opens the door a sliver and then a little farther. Rumpled sheets and nothing more.

But the lights are on.

"Mama?" she whispers. She goes to the closet, but it is empty, too.

"It's so late," she says. And then she knows she must check one more place. A place that haunts her, even in her dreams, and the coffee can becomes a heavy weight but not heavy enough to keep her feet from moving to the bathroom. She is tired. She doesn't want to go. She has looked too many times, and she doesn't want to look anymore. It makes her crazy, and she probably is, she *is*, to let it hold on to her, to clamp down on her like a trap that is sprung over and over again, but, *keep an eye on her, Zoe, watch out for her, where is she, where is she, where the fucking hell is she?*

And she tears back the shower curtain to see an empty white bathtub.

Nothing more.

She clutches the coffee can, her fingers running up and down the ridges like she is calming Kyle by rubbing his head, like she is rubbing the fear right out of him.

Except for the muffled strum of her fingers against metal, the house is still, quiet, but then she hears another sound, this one coming from deep within. A rumbling furrow slides through her soul, sliding into her brain, a furrow that separates one part of her heart from the other.

And then it is quiet again.

SEVENTEEN

Sounds echo around her, heavy and dull, like she is underwater.

Is this, she wonders, *what it is like to be dead?* To be vaguely aware of flesh and breathing and feet scraping across a floor, but not to be a part of it? To be invisible to the mortals surrounding you, isolated in your front-seat coffin desk, forgotten and slowly, slowly curling into your dead world and forgetting about them, too? The bell rings, and the scraping reaches a frenzy as feet rush out the door, away, away from Mrs. Garrett, who rules the living. Zoe remains seated and lifts unblinking eyes to Mrs. Garrett, who is a glacier before her. It is a whisper, a quiet act of defiance that says, I still breathe. Mrs. Garrett maintains the tilt of her head, observes her domain, her eyes rigid on the depleting landscape, full of control and awareness, but eyes never straying to Zoe, who is just a few inches below her nose. A few lousy inches. Invisible. *Bitch,* Zoe thinks. *Fucking bitch.* Zoe leaves the classroom, her own feet scuffling and echoing in her ears in a distant, dead way, and she can feel Mrs. Garrett's satisfaction burning a hole in her back.

Her throat is dry, cracked. No words have passed her lips in the last hour. And now comes Group, where all they will want her to do is talk and cry and spill her guts, and that is the last thing she wants to do there. Maybe now she can answer the question Mrs. Garrett asked—the question Zoe raised her hand for, but because she is invisible Mrs. Garrett called on the person next to her, behind her, the one walking down the hall, the one in the next town, anyone but Zoe. Zoe, who doesn't exist. How can you hear someone who doesn't exist?

And now they want her to talk? Fucking fat chance. She wants to throw her head back and laugh so loudly the irony ricochets all the way back to Mrs. Farantino's office. But her throat is too dry for more than a pathetic croak. And now she is missing Friday P.E., where alliances are being made, shots are being practiced, and coaches are watching before practice even begins. But they won't be watching Zoe. Invisible again. Shit. She is really going to like Group.

Group is held in Room 10A, a portable with a rickety ramp on the outermost edge of the campus. She smiles. *Maybe they are afraid of us cursing types,* she thinks. *Keep us far away from the noncursers. We could be dangerous.* The loud pinging of the rusty steel ramp announces her arrival, and she holds off opening the door. She had wanted to slip in quietly and sit in the back unnoticed. Now every eye will be on her. Her throat feels like it is sticking to itself and could seal shut with one more dry breath. She tries to muster some saliva to soothe the dryness, but her mouth won't cooperate. *Shit. Let 'em look.* She opens the door.

The room is empty.

She steps back out and looks at the number on the door: 10A. She digs the counseling agreement out of her notebook; 10A is circled in red at the top. *This is going to be easy,* she thinks, and she steps back in.

"That's right—10A. You got it. Come on in. You Zoe Buckman?"

She searches for the voice and finally sees a man at a table in the corner, almost hidden by stacks of papers and books. His hair is frosty white, and heavy glasses are sliding down his sweaty nose. He stands, and she sees a large belly pressed tight against a white buttoned shirt. His sleeves are rolled up to his elbows, and he holds out a palm indicating that she should sit.

She stays near the door. "I think there's a mistake. I am supposed to be here for some kind of group session."

"No mistake. You're it. The first week of school is slim pickings. We don't usually have anyone this soon, in fact. So for now you get my full attention."

Her stomach pinches like it has been folded in half. There will be no sliding into the back. There will be no listening to others. No fading out after a couple of sessions. Only her. Could life get worse? It should be Mama, or Grandma, or Mrs. Garrett sitting here being looked at under a microscope.

Not her. Not for one lousy cussword, when they have spent a lifetime screwing up lives.

His palm waves again, and she sits. She sits for fifty minutes, and they listen to him wheeze, listen to the buttons on his too-tight shirt scrape the edge of the table, listen to the air conditioner click on and off, and then more wheezing and throat-clearing. For this she is missing P.E. For this she is slipping from fourth, to fifth, or tenth, or maybe dead last.

He prompts her. He prods. He discusses his hobbies. He discusses his name—Mr. K, because his full name is too long and difficult to pronounce. He asks her about her name. Simple ploy, she thinks. She grunts and nods and shrugs, strains to keep the conversation going, to keep from using a word that might turn his ears pink, too. She doesn't want her sentence extended. She wants to be paroled. She wants the hell out of there. Her stomach rumbles. She skipped lunch to ration out her money. Five dollars and a can of pennies won't go far. And then out of nowhere a thought lodges in her brain, *Did Mama eat the Chinese in the fridge?* Without Zoe prompting her, has she eaten anything at all? *Mama.* The bell rings, and the thought dissolves. She stands to leave. Mr. K stands, too.

"Zoe," he says, not to her but to the air, like he is trying it out. "Zoe." He pushes his glasses back on his nose. "An interesting name." *Another obvious ploy,* she thinks. *Pathetic.* But she likes hearing her name pass from someone else's lips. His voice is deep and buttery, almost like Daddy's. "Means 'life,' doesn't it?" Zoe nods, trying to conceal her surprise. Mr. K holds his hand out, and she reluctantly takes it. "Nice talking to you," he says. "See you next week."

"Sure," she answers, but hopes she won't see him next week or ever again.

She slips out the door and pings down the ramp, but still, she can't help but be impressed that he knew about her name. Not many people would know something like that. The last person who had ever even mentioned it was Aunt Nadine. It was after Daddy's funeral, in the parking lot of Ruby First Baptist. Aunt Nadine lifted Zoe's face with both of her hands and peered into it like she was holding a treasure.

"Look at those eyes," she said. "Just like your daddy's. That was always my favorite thing about him. So big and dark you can just melt into them." Zoe didn't answer. "And he did a mighty fine job choosing your name, too. It means 'full of life.' Did you know that, Zoe?"

Zoe had only nodded, and wishes now she had done something more meaningful, something more than a nod to show Aunt Nadine how deep her words had gone, how much they had filled her when she was feeling so empty. Grateful. She was grateful beyond any telling for those few words Aunt Nadine had offered. She *was* grateful, but she had never said so.

Zoe hasn't seen her Aunt Nadine since the funeral. She wonders about her aunt, Brownsville, and how far away they both are from Ruby. So far. *Maybe just far enough,* she thinks.

By the time she makes it all the way to the other side of

campus and changes into her tennis clothes, almost everyone has been assigned a court. She fastens her hair back in a ponytail as she approaches the small group that remains.

"You're late," the coach says.

"Barely," Zoe answers.

"Enough," he says.

He sends her to the last court to play singles with Doreen Stark. Doreen. The syrupy secret pal queen of niceness and giggles who cannot return a ball hit with a force above a baby's burp.

Formalities are honored. They shake hands. Doreen smiles, giggles, bounces back to position. Zoe watches her rock back and forth like she is ready to slam the ball. It is all for show, but Zoe does not play for show. She plays to win. It is the one thing she can do. The one place where the control is hers. She loses, it's her fault. She can take that. She wins, it's her skill. She can take that, too.

Doreen turns and waves to her mother in the bleachers. Some parents not only come to games, they come to practice, too. Zoe has never had anyone to turn and wave to, but she shakes the thought away. Tennis is able to do that for her. With each bounce of the ball in front of her, her focus narrows. She serves the first ball and aces it in the corner. Doreen's swing comes hours too late. Doreen shrugs and smiles and bounces to the other side to wait for the next serve. Zoe eases up on her serves, wanting some play and a chance to practice her backhand. The game still ends forty–love, and Zoe has not broken a sweat. The next game ends the same. Doreen smiles and giggles, and her mom cheers her on despite the loss. The coach moves Zoe up a court to play Annie Meacham, and when she wins again, up another court to play Libby Wheeler. By the end of the two-hour practice, she is at the first court playing doubles with the best players on the team.

She runs, swings, and smashes until the sweet, orangy scent of her body is gathering in droplets, running in streams down her temples and soaking her back. She has heard that sweating is a way to get the poisons out of your body. With each swing, each grunt of air expelled from her lungs, she thinks it must be true. Poison seems to drain from her as she smashes the ball with the pent-up force inside. She and her partner lose the match, but just barely. It was close—the victors know that—and it brings Zoe satisfaction. No one may be cheering her from the bleachers, but the joy of an almost-victory is enough. The coach pats her on the back and tells her not to be late for their first competition in the morning. The bus leaves at seven.

He gathers everyone around for a last-minute pep talk and to introduce the new assistant coach, who arrived late. *If you're over twenty-one, I guess it's okay to be late,* Zoe thinks.

"And don't forget, your transportation fees have to be paid to the finance office by the end of next week," he says. "It's gone up this year to forty-five dollars."

A flash of adrenaline pierces her chest. She did forget.

Every year they have to pay it. The school doesn't cover optional activities. And it doesn't matter if they take the lousy bus or not, they still have to fork over the bucks. Forty-five dollars by next week. Do football players have to pay their own way? she wants to ask. She is going to have to perform magic with her tips to have the money by then. She gets her paycheck from Murray next Friday—but that would be after school—too late. She swings her racket over her shoulder, and heads for the locker room. She'll figure it out somehow. She'll go home to her room and count the pennies. Her room. No excuses. She's had enough of them. *Make it work, Zoe.*

But how? she wonders. She showers. She stuffs damp, stinky clothes into her bag. And then she throws her racket into the back of the Thunderbird that is already down to a quarter of a tank.

* ⁺ ₊

She stops at Taco Shack, where tacos are two for a dollar and soda refills are free. Her hands shake as she orders. She sits alone, the fluorescent light flattening her against the booth. The tacos are small, and after two she is still hungry. She drinks more soda and refills again before she leaves, and once more an unwanted thought slices through her concentration. Mama loves tacos. Should she take her one? But the answer is no. Of course, no. One or two tacos will not change Mama. They barely keep her own stomach from rumbling. And Mama's hunger runs deeper than a dozen tacos could reach.

EIGHTEEN

Metal against metal. The scrape of her key in the lock has a peeling effect, like layers of tight clothing being torn away. Mama. Money. Grandma. Until she is down to lightness. The room. Like tennis. A corner of control. Forward. Future. She enters into her space and soaks in the clean, the polish, the humming refrigerator, the fading shafts of light. The order.

The panther's faint tick floats across silence. Six-fifteen. She told the twins she would come to their sister's *Quinceañera* tonight. She remembers back to Monica's fifteenth birthday. Half of Ruby seemed to be there. The party was rolled out from the backyard to the front, and the overflow spilled out to the street. And there was lots of food. Tables of food.

She will go.

But before she leaves she must do laundry. She only has one tennis skirt, and she needs it for her match in the morning. She pulls off one sock and then the other, her feet hot on the cool, polished floor. She pauses, startled, but absorbed in the simple sensation of her feet on a smooth, clean floor. She looks around the room. Is it really hers? Clean. Empty of past. She sits on the window seat and props her feet on a lavender pillow. Before laundry, before anything, she needs to sit. She needs to be. Just be. She closes her eyes, leaning back against the alcove. Zoe. Zoe listening to evening chirps through an open window. Zoe fingering a golden tassel. Zoe tasting space. Zoe owning the room. Zoe, owning her life. She is not invisible. Zoe asking and answering questions that are all her own. Her thoughts come in no particular order, some questions, some observations, none pressing, like a meandering stroll that still has destination. Breaths and half-thoughts barely fill the crevices in between.

Will I win my match tomorrow?

   leg   *stubble*

My nails look like shit.

      my room

       tell Carly   *Reid too*

What was that book guy reading? Did he notice me at all?

         who

I wonder   *what is Mr. K's "difficult" name?*

        laundry   *only my laundry*

Pick up Kyle's gift at the kite shop.

   breeze   *jasmine*   *or is it honeysuckle?*

       my window   *mine*

     a lavender pillow for my feet

Kyle should see this

Should I take a salad to his party? Something?

count the pennies

My legs need shaving.

Mama

Have I always had that white dot on my shin?

a white freckle? a star on my shin

What made Opal paint stars on the ceiling?

my room   mine

Could taxes make her lose her house?

Does she have anyone besides the Count?

Anyone at all?

A sparrow lands on the sill just inches from Zoe—so close, except for the thin pane of glass separating them. She holds her breath, not wanting it to fly away, but it sees the furtive movement of her eyes and its wings beat a line of retreat, carrying the moment and Zoe's questions with it.

She stands, stretches, pulls her tennis skirt and team T-shirt from her gym bag, and then with a second glance gathers more laundry until her arms are full. Opal told her she was welcome to use the laundry room. She hopes that includes laundry detergent since she has none. Would shampoo work? She shakes her head. Probably not. She remembers putting a bottle of green dish soap in the washing machine when she was ten. Suds oozed everywhere and left a sticky mess on the clothes. But she was only ten. No one told her or showed her how to use a washing machine. She had to figure it out herself.

She walks down the hall, the floorboards creaking beneath her bare feet. She has never gone beyond her bathroom at the head of the stairs except for the night she moved in. She hopes it is all right to go to the laundry room this way. Opal said the washer and dryer were on the covered screen porch. She also remembers that is where Count Basil spends most of his time. He was friendly enough the night she met him, but without Opal by her side would he be just as inclined to take off a leg or two for an afternoon snack? He could. His neck is as massive as a tree trunk.

The house is quiet. She wonders where Opal is. Dancing with birds? She makes her way to the back, past the kitchen, and then past three other closed doors that she can only wonder about. More sabers behind them? Or another snarling grizzly? Or maybe something as innocent as yellow snapdragons? She cautiously pushes open the screen door that leads to the porch with her hip and tries to see around her armful of laundry.

She stops.

Count Basil stares at her. Foam oozes from his black mouth. His lips are pulled back, exposing his canines. His eyes are unblinking, and his nose twitches. Zoe cannot hold back and erupts into laughter, snorting through her nose. Seeing him flinch makes another laugh roll from her belly. It comes out as a surprise and feels almost cleansing. He doesn't move, though Zoe is sure she can detect some level of humiliation in his eyes.

"Ah! You laugh, but look at 'em! He's got 'em all, with minty breath, too. Not bad for an old fart like him. He may find himself a lady friend yet." Opal pulls back the lip on the left side of his mouth and continues to brush his teeth. Drops of foam sprinkle the floor. The Count obediently waits for her to finish. "I know he don't care for it much when it's getting done, but afterwards he seems to smile more."

Zoe grins. Is that what you call it? A smile? Grandma would call him "mad dog" and phone the pound. Zoe leans down and picks up her fallen laundry.

"You said it was okay to use the washer?"

"Sure is." Opal grunts as she wrestles the dog, who Zoe guesses must easily outweigh the old woman by fifty pounds. "There!" she says, dropping the toothbrush in the laundry tub with one hand and slapping the Count on the backside with the other. He takes it as a signal to run, and he nearly knocks Zoe over as he races down the steps to the backyard.

Opal straightens, pushing against her back like it helps in the effort. "Here. Let me show you how it works." Before Zoe can say anything, Opal is scooping a cup of detergent into the washer and turning on faucets, showing her with pride all there is to know about the Zenith Ultra, model 750. She shows Zoe the settings, the bleach dispenser, and then the lint trap to the dryer. "I have a clothesline, too. Like it better, nothing like sunshine dried right into your clothes, but it twitches out my back lifting all that wet laundry, so these days I mostly stick with the canned air. But you're welcome to use either—or both if it suits you."

Zoe smiles. Why would she use both? She begins stuffing her clothes into the washer, and Opal stops her. "What's this? A *tennis* skirt?"

Oh my god, Zoe thinks. *Is she going to inspect all my dirty laundry?* "Yes," she answers and hopes Opal won't see her sweat-stained, threadbare bra lurking somewhere in the pile.

Opal sits down in a wicker chair next to the dryer and brushes a silver curl from her forehead. "So you play tennis?" Her voice is soft and grateful, like she is settling into a warm bathtub, or maybe, Zoe thinks, settling into warm memories.

"I'm on the team at school. I have a match in the morning—that's why I have to get the skirt clean tonight."

"The team!" Opal's eyes glitter, and Zoe catches her breath. What is that? Excitement? Admiration? What is in Opal's eyes? Zoe drops the last of her clothes into the washer and closes the lid. She looks back at Opal's eyes, and the glitter is still there.

"Yes. Varsity." Zoe listens to her own voice and wonders at the low, hesitant pitch, but then she knows—it is fear creeping up in her. For two years she has either gotten no reaction from Mama or ridicule from Grandma when it comes to her tennis. Her defenses automatically ease into position, but still . . . the glitter.

"So you play *tomorrow,*" Opal says, stretching out the word like there is magic in it. She leans back. "I was on a team once," she says. "About a hundred years ago. Calvin and I played in a doubles league. Boy, did we have some fun—and how I loved wearing that tiny pleated skirt. Calvin liked it, too." Opal winks.

"Calvin?"

"That was my husband. Is my husband. Well, he's dead you know, but that don't make him stop being my husband. But it surely pisses me off that he left first. He was pretty much that way though."

Zoe doesn't know whether to laugh or express sorrow. Opal always seems to be throwing her curves. The washing machine finishes filling and begins its low, churning rhythm, while Opal continues her excited chatter, saving Zoe the decision to express anything at all.

"We played once a week—all over the county. It was a club for couples—nothing fancy—but Calvin and I could sure serve some firecrackers. Of course, Calvin had to do ninety percent of the running. I wasn't much good at that, not with my bum leg and all."

"Bum leg?" Zoe asks.

Opal smiles. "You didn't notice?" She seems pleased and pulls up her long, loose house dress to expose her shoes. One has a normal thin sole, the other a thick, heavy one. "Three full inches shorter, this one!" She lowers her dress like a curtain ending a show. "But I don't let it slow me down much. Couldn't keep me from tennis!" She slaps her hands on her knees and stands. "So, Miss Zoe Beth Buckman, ace tennis player. Now that I've shown you the washer, let's go take a look at your plot of garden." She slides her arm through Zoe's and pulls her down the porch steps to the yard.

Zoe tries to remember. Plot of garden? She remembers something was said about it, but it hadn't been important to her. She doesn't garden. She doesn't want to garden. But she doesn't want to be rude or ungrateful either. Not ungrateful. So she lets Opal pull her along in the twilight garden as Count Basil lollops behind, smiling. She will let Opal show her. What can it hurt? And she likes the alert, steady rhythm of Opal's chatter, so much the timbre of a warbling bird that it folds into the evening air as naturally as Zoe's breaths.

NINETEEN

The purple dahlias have no scent, but the earthy tang of their leaves and freshly cut stems fills the car. Opal tied them together with a piece of raffia, and Zoe is grateful that she has a gift to offer Yolanda for her *Quinceañera*. The bundle is impressive—each bloom twice the size of Zoe's palm—and the petals are prickly fresh, with white edging the purple. When she admired them in the garden she didn't expect Opal to start cutting them for her. She thinks about her plot of dirt. Why would Opal suggest such a thing? She only wanted a room. But now the idea is taking root in her in a strange way she didn't expect, like seeds tossed out that sprout in spite of neglect. A garden. Maybe she could plant dahlias, too. Or maybe cabbages? Who would have thought cabbages could be beautiful? But when Opal proudly showed off the cabbages in her garden, Zoe had to reach down and run her fingers across the thick, ruffled leaves. The only cabbages Zoe had ever seen before were hard, pale green balls. Opal's were clothed as uniquely as she was—flowing leafy ruffles of purple, yellow, and deep green. *Cabbages or dahlias, definitely.*

The streets of Ruby are dark. She rolls down a window and lights a cigarette. She pulls in deeply. She used the last of her cash to buy a new pack. A foolish thing, maybe, but tonight she will be able to eat at the party and probably take a handful of cookies and a soda with her for breakfast in the morning. And tomorrow after tennis is Kyle's party, where she will be able to eat again. Aunt Patsy makes lasagna to die for. Or maybe Uncle Clint will barbecue. Her stomach twists. The tiny tacos are long since gone. And then on Sunday she works and can eat again. It's working. It is. She takes another puff and flicks the ashes out the window. It wasn't foolish to buy the cigarettes. She watches the needle of the gas gauge point lower. *You only sling hash. You'll never make it.* And she still needs the transportation fees. And then there is the next month's rent coming. She feels the comfort of the room leaving her. She has only had it three days and already feels it slipping from her grasp. But she will never go crawling back. *Do you hear that, Grandma? Never.*

And there is always the can of pennies. She has no choice. Living with Mama . . . dying with Mama . . . being nothing with Mama . . . and now with Daddy gone . . .

Her thoughts are drawn to the aqueduct. What would it be like to walk the beams at night? With blackness above and below her. Blackness everywhere. You would hardly know where to step. The thought frightens her, but she allows it to coil about her like a snake around her ankles. Dangerous. Deadly. But exciting. At night. All alone. All darkness. *Daddy, what would happen? What does it feel like?*

She slows and turns at the 7-Eleven. Monica and Jorge live in a neighborhood on the border of Ruby and Duborn. Their house is a small white clapboard on a narrow street that is always crowded with cars even when there is no party. She figures she will probably have to park a street or two over and hike. She's over an hour late, so the party is probably well under way.

"Quinceañera," she whispers aloud, because she likes the sensual roll of the word on her tongue. Fifteen. Zoe can't remember her fifteenth birthday. She tries to think back. Her birthday is in August. Daddy was still alive then—he didn't die until October of that year. But her birthday—that is a blur. No, not a blur, just a day like any other. The novelty of children and birthdays had long since faded by then for Mama and Daddy. The hobby was forgotten. Her sixteenth she remembers. That was when she and Reid—when they—was it really that long ago?

She hasn't been with anyone since—over a year now. Being with Reid changed things for her. She squints, as if the glare of the memory hurts her eyes. She used Reid, the way she had been used. It meant something to him. It meant less than nothing to her.

It started with needing to be touched by someone,

anyone. More than touched. Loved. Daddy was the only who had touched her, stroked her hair, told her how special she was. Brief moments as he left to drink with his buddies or before he went to bed with Mama with a beer in his hand. Brief moments, but they were *there. Glitter, Zoe. Stars, Zoe. Special.*

She looked for that recognition after he died—it was obvious even to her. He left a hole, a missing piece in an already faded, barely held together puzzle. She needed to hold it together in some way. If she could just get a small part of him back. Some way. She thought she had found it with a jerk whose brain stem hung between his legs. But it was always about his needs and never about hers. His name was Jaime, with the emphasis on *me.* She thought she found it again a month later with a "sensitive poet," who surprisingly lost his muse once his words had whittled their way to their intended target. And then there was a jock whose face she barely remembers. He never looked into her eyes. Not once. Then came a couple of others who were just as forgettable. And then Reid. He was just there. And she didn't care. By then she just didn't care. She wanted to see what it was like when you didn't care.

It would be easier if he hated her, but he is still her friend, maybe more, and that makes it worse—that and the fact that Carly doesn't know. It's an ugly secret that gnaws at her.

She finds a parking space one street over and gathers up

the flowers along with her handmade card. She can hear the music already, floating over rooftops on the warm evening air. It promises people, crowds, talking, and the impossibility of being alone. The houses she passes are tiny and dark, but then as she turns onto Monica and Jorge's street, the crowds begin forming. A few in front of this house, a few more in front of another, and by the time she gets to their little white clapboard, the street and the yard are full. Strings of tiny colored lights hang from trees, are woven through front porch lattice, and shimmy down from rooftop to gatepost to create a lighted entrance through the driveway to the backyard. She doesn't recognize the mixture of faces, but with six brothers and sisters with circles of their own friends and a dozen aunts and uncles and half a neighborhood that was probably invited, she suspects she won't know most of those here. Yolanda is the youngest—the last *Quinceañera*. Being the last had to mean something, Zoe thinks, when they were stringing the lights and spreading the word.

She walks across the mat of lawn, up the steps, and in through the open front door. Elbow to elbow, she says hi to Monica's mother and then to Abuelita, her tiny shriveled grandmother, who is always smiling. Abuelita speaks no English. She doesn't need to, Zoe thinks. Her smile fills and communicates so much more than the empty, half-said words of Zoe's life. She pushes through the kitchen to the backyard, where she sees Yolanda—and food.

"Happy Birthday," Zoe says, laying the bundle in Yolanda's arms and kissing her cheek. The music is loud, and they yell a few greetings to each other. Then Yolanda is pulled away by her friends, and Zoe is alone again. Where is Monica? Carly? From behind she feels a tug and turns around. Jorge and Reid both wear sloppy grins.

"You finally made it," Jorge says. "The party started two hours ago. We're way ahead of you." His pupils are large, his smile dreamy. Zoe sniffs the contents of his red plastic cup.

"Way ahead," she answers. "I'm just interested in food. Come with me while I fix a plate." But they say no, they are going to go dance, and they melt into elbows and faces and music that is spinning a step ahead of Zoe. *Food,* she thinks, *I just need food.* She slinks to a picnic table and three card tables loaded with colorful casseroles, salads, and desserts and begins filling a plate. By the time she reaches the end of the last table, her plate is piled high enough for two people. She is embarrassed and finds a dark corner to eat—at least until the pile is smaller. She takes two cookies and a churro from her plate, wraps them in a napkin and slides them into her purse, hoping no one notices her in the shadows.

She leans back against the fence and in her dark corner alternates between spoonfuls of rice and a spicy fajita whose peppers burn her tongue. The heat simmers in her throat and stomach, and she wipes a line of sweat from her hair-line. She sips her Coke to ease the burn and eats some more. She lifts another forkful of rice to her mouth and catches a glimpse of Carly dancing with Derek Riley and then the crowd swallows them up and spits out a glimpse of Reid and Jody Simmons. There is the brief sway of Monica before she, too, is folded back into the mass. *It's alive,* Zoe thinks. It fascinates her, this throbbing, pulsing mass, electrified beneath the patio arbor by twinkling lights, a breathing, beating mass she watches from the shadows, alone.

And then another familiar face is flagged before her eyes and just as quickly disappears, but not before her plate tips and half the food tumbles to the grass. She stands, searching for another glimpse.

Who is that?

Zoe feels the rush of the crowd come out to meet her, and a ripple of its life runs through her veins. Her heart speeds its pace. She eats a few more quick mouthfuls and abandons the rest of her plate on the end of the picnic table. She slides into the edge of the crowd, straining her neck, dancing her way between Carly and Monica. Carly's throat shines with perspiration, and wet curls cling to her face. Monica, always efficient, has her hair pulled in a knot on her head, and a wet napkin in her hand wipes away the frenzy of the dance. Zoe hugs. She says hello. But then she strains for more.

And she sees it.

She jabs Monica in the ribs and says between tightly drawn lips and downcast eyes. "Who is that?"

"Who?" Monica says much too loudly.

"There." She glances with her eyes, and Monica follows them.

"Him? He came with my brother Vic. His name's Carlos, I think." And Monica twirls back into her own world, just as Zoe leaves it. She works her way over to him. He is not at someone else's station now, and she is not clocked in on anyone else's time but her own. Mostly she wants to see if she is remotely more interesting than a book. Her chest burns, and she wonders if it is only the peppers. Monica's brother is twenty-two. Is he, too? He has stopped dancing. His toasted-almond skin glistens in the dim light, and a small, damp triangle marks his thin white T-shirt. He leans against a post with a beer in one hand.

"Where's your book?" she blurts out, and then in the same instant wishes she had stayed safely in the shadows. She prays to be back in the shadows. Her voice is too loud. Too blunt. What insanity pushed her across the yard to just a breath away from someone she doesn't know and doesn't want to know in the first place? But now she must politely wait for his answer to her ridiculous question before she fades back to her safe darkness.

He studies her for a moment and asks, "Where's your apron?"

So he did notice her. His voice is soft and slow. Warmth spreads in rivers through her belly, and she forgets about leaving. They talk. It comes easy, like a sigh or a swallow or a stroll through a garden with an old woman at twilight.

"You read a lot?" she asks.

"Right now I do. I'm studying to be a paramedic—applying to the Abilene Fire Department next month. And if I don't get hired there, I've heard they're hiring at Fort Worth."

"So you want to stay close?"

"What good would life be without Murray's chicken-fried steak? But I'll go where I have to."

"They're not hiring in Ruby?"

He grunts. Question answered.

"I guess Ruby isn't exactly the job capital of the world."

"You like working at Murray's?"

"What's not to like? Good food, nice boss, and great customers who are big tippers."

He laughs. "Pressure's on now."

"You got it."

They walk to the coolers, and he takes a soda out for her. She holds the icy can to her cheek. They talk about Ruby, cars, music, and, finally, their names.

"How'd you get a name like Carlos O'Malley?"

"Same way everyone does. My parents. The O'Malley came without saying. My dad's Irish, but my mom wanted some of her heritage in there, too—and my grandfather's name is Carlos. So I got a little from both sides." *Both sides.* Zoe wonders. Did she? She has Daddy's dark looks, but is there anything in her like Mama? Did she get something from both of them? Or when she was that little unwanted peanut in Mama's tummy, did she grow all on her own even then, without any help from Mama?

They walk together through the shadows, talking about the opportunities in Ruby. "When I turned twenty-one a few months ago, I knew I had to start looking beyond Ruby. I don't want to spend my life dropping orange cones on the Texas road crew. My brother's a fireman in Austin. Loves his job. Has a family. Two little kids. And that's what—" He stops. "This is probably boring the hell out of you. You came to a party for more than an update on the job prospects of a cone dropper." He sets his beer on nearby fence post. "Want to dance?"

She nods and they step the few feet to the lighted arbor and squeeze onto the square of cement.

He stands close. They dance. They circle. But they keep some distance. *I don't need this,* she thinks. *My life's too complicated already.* But his eyes linger in hers, and she lets them. It spreads fire through her. Warmth she wants to settle into. But she is wary, too. She hasn't judged well in the past. A complete failure, more like it. *Maybe this time is different.* She sways, draws closer, teeters near an edge no one else can see, but then another turn and she sees Reid watching from a distance. Reid. Leaning. Focused. Watching. The fire turns to shame. She is suddenly cold. Her thoughts jam up. No thinking. No talking. Just leaving. All she can think of is to leave and the words trip from her mouth. "I—I have to go."

"I'll walk you to your car," Carlos answers, but she knows Reid would see that, too. Reid would think—she knows what he would think—and he probably wouldn't be wrong.

"No," she says, but a few feet away, she turns and sees Reid is blocked out again by the shifting mass of dancing bodies. It's an opening, a brief secret exit, and she says, "Okay." They walk and they talk and they lean against her car for another hour, but nothing happens because she is still afraid, and she senses he is, too. She reads his eyes and knows there has been trouble somewhere, sometime, and somehow she frightens him, which makes her want him that much more. Her insides burn, with need or fajitas, she isn't sure. Maybe both.

"I have to go," she finally says, and he nods like he knows the time is right.

+ *
 +

She leaves, squeezing through narrow streets bulging with parked cars, down the glaring, lighted thoroughfare of Main, with the faint scent of the dahlias still lingering in the car and the stronger scent of solitude sweeping over her. Alone again.

The Thunderbird is a dark vacuum, an airless space light-years from everything. She fights an impulse to drive by her house and shake Mama, shake her over and over, shake her until a part of Zoe shakes right out and Zoe picks it up and runs. And the impulse shifts to a burning urge to drive to Grandma's tiny apartment and bang on her cold, bolted heart, to go to Aunt Patsy's and Uncle Clint's and beg to be worthy like Kyle, to go back to the party and dance with Carlos even if Reid is watching, dance close and hot until their sweat runs together, because his eyes and his mouth and everything about him makes her burn, but instead she keeps her hands steady on the wheel, steady, all the way to her room on Lorelei Street. When she gets there she changes her clothes, turns out the light, and crawls between light sheets cooled by a thin breeze.

But still she burns. She is on fire with need. Burning that goes deeper than her skin, etched deeply, maybe in her soul, and there seems to be nothing for it, no balm, save inching her arms up to hold herself and wishing the arms weren't her own.

TWENTY

Sweat mingles with tears. Tiny tears. Tears that no one sees. No one knows. But Zoe. She feels each one. She feels them trickle like sweat, but different because they start in her heart, wind through her throat, and then spring from the corners of her eyes like birth. It feels like birth. New. She wipes them away, like sweat, and no one knows but her. She knows.

"Deuce!" She swings. Not just a swing. A death serve. The serve is missed, and a cheer and a bark roar from a tiny spot in the crowd that seems to Zoe to fill all of Ruby.

"Ad-in!" Her next serve slams into the corner but is returned. Her backhand hisses the ball back through the air, kissing the net. It is her last game. Singles. She won her doubles match. Singles are reserved for the strongest players. Sometimes she plays, sometimes not. Today she's up against the number-two player at Cooper Springs High. Her next return is low—too low. It hits the net and falls back on her side. But still, another cheer and a long-tongued smile. And she swipes at the sweat-tears again.

"Deuce!" The ball slices the air and the green and the lines, and the Cooper Springs player shakes her head at a ball she hardly saw.

Another cheer, and Zoe fights to keep the tiny unnoticed tears from growing into a sob.

"Ad-in!" The serve bullets into the hot spot, and the ball is returned but sails out of court.

"Game Buckman!" the referee calls.

And the air and sound stop. For Zoe. Movement is syrup slow, stretching out thin.

Slow, while she turns.

For the first time ever, she turns and waves into the bleachers. She waves at someone who is waving back at her. A crazy, cheering, silver-haired lady with a pom-pom, a flag, and a smiling dog.

In the bleachers.

For Zoe.

TWENTY-ONE

"I didn't know you were coming," Zoe says. It is awkward. She doesn't know if she should say thank you. She doesn't want to say thank you. It seems too . . . needy. She thought about it on her way home. She thought about it as she showered and changed. It pulled and it twisted until a light thought became heavy. Why would Opal *want* to come? For *her*? And now as she runs down the stairs to go to Kyle's party, Opal and Count Basil are there bringing in the mail, and something must be said. "It's just that I was surprised is all."

Opal hugs her mail to her chest and tweaks her head to the side in her sparrowlike way. "Really, dear? You didn't read it?" she asks, smiling.

Read it? Zoe skims back through her mind and days.

"My eyes, dear. I thought you read my eyes yesterday. I read the invitation in yours."

I invited her? I have to be careful with my eyes, Zoe thinks. *She might read all kinds of things there. What is she reading now?* Zoe looks down and picks at her cuticle. "Sure," she says. And then she looks back up but is still afraid, a gauzy, thin familiar feeling circles her mouth holding back words that she does and doesn't want to say. Words that might open a wound that is just scabbing over.

"You're welcome!" Opal says, her words breathy and soft. "And I thank you! You were amazing! The Count and I had such a time!"

Opal goes back to sifting through her mail and grimaces. "Bills!" she says. And then the smile returns like a bird that can't be shooed from a nest. "Maybe if I change the name to Opal's Lorelei Home for the Criminally Insane it would keep them away!" Always possibility.

Zoe smiles. "Thank you, Opal."

And it doesn't seem needy at all.

+ *
+

She leaves, letting Opal's criminally insane possibilities entertain her as she drives and appreciating Opal's concern over bills. No excuses. Humor, but no excuses. Mama never even looked at the mail.

Mama.

Will she be there today?

Zoe knows no one is expecting her, except maybe Kyle. Kyle will be looking for Zoe. But Grandma will have made it known that she was uninvited. Mama, Aunt Patsy, Uncle Clint—they all will know. Will they want her there?

And then an icy thought catches her, starkly, in the middle of the Indian summer heat. It's been four days since she left home and, other than Grandma, no one has tried to see what happened to her. Hasn't Mama even wanted to come see her? Make sure she is okay? Wondered about her suspension at school? Wondered about anything at all? Or is it still just about Mama? Mama, and how everything affects her. Never about Zoe.

Or maybe it is simply that there is no part of "Mama" left. No part that Zoe remembers. No part that held her hand in the grocery store. That smoothed her hair away from her face with spit-moistened fingers. That painted Zoe's toenails in rainbow colors and then laughed as they wiggled. And now Zoe questions those memories, too. How real were they? As fuzzy as her memories of running through a sprinkler on a hot Texas day when it seemed that Shasta daisies were crowding for room near the porch and Popsicles filled the freezer. How much was real . . . and how much was wanting?

There has always been wanting. Wanting her clothes to be washed and pressed with love. Wanting someone to pack her a lunch. Wanting someone to double-check her school papers. Wanting someone to meet her at the bus. Wanting someone to care if her socks matched or her underwear were clean or her teeth brushed. Zoe did all those things for Kyle. The wanting told her to do it for him.

She stops at Barry's Hobby Shop on Third Street and picks up the kite she ordered for Kyle two months ago. Thank God she'd already paid for it all or she'd be stuck. "Forty-nine dollars," she sighs, thinking how much gas, food, and cigarettes that could buy. But she didn't know then where she would be now, and two months ago when she saw the kite, she knew she had to get it for him. Kiteman, she has called him since he was four and stretched his arms to the sky trying to touch the tails with his hopeful stubby fingers. From digging holes with spoons to throwing balls for Zoe to chasing kite tails, Kyle found his own ways to pass time waiting for Daddy to return to the park to get them. The Dragonslayer 1000 is incredibly beautiful, even to Zoe—with its iridescent emerald diamonds on a shimmering blue background and its spinning tails of forest green—plus, she splurged on a rubber-gripped reel that could wind in the massive kite with ease. She can't wait to see Kyle's face when he opens it. Did he know about her leaving? He is only ten—no, eleven now. Would Grandma put Zoe's leaving on his shoulders, or would she keep it among the adults and spare him the worry? Of course, when it comes to Mama, no one is spared. "He'll know," she whispers.

Zoe turns on the last road out of Cooper Springs into the subdivision where Uncle Clint and Aunt Patsy live. Their double-wide home is still more than a mile off, but she can already see it peeking up on a small rise in the landscape. It is a green postage stamp in the cracked bareness. A sparse sprinkling of other homes dot the area as well, but Uncle Clint has a heavy hand with watering and planting, and poplars shoot up in the distance like giant green geysers, setting his house apart from the others.

An oasis, she thinks. Uncle Clint's Double-Wide Oasis.

Her insides flutter as she gets closer, and she thinks for a moment to have another quick smoke before she gets there, but as her fingers rummage blindly through her purse on the seat next to her, she realizes there isn't time. Shit. *Shit*. She takes several quick breaths instead, trying to will the tension away. She turns into the long gravel drive and counts the parked cars already there. Aunt Patsy's, Uncle Clint's, Grandma's, and two others she doesn't recognize. She wishes there were more, like at Yolanda's party. Hundreds more so she could dissolve into other faces and conversations. But she already knows that Kyle's party will be nothing like Yolanda's.

Her car crunches to a stop on the loose gray gravel, and the sound of her slamming car door rattles the still air. She knows everyone is probably around on the back patio under the shade of the aluminum awning, but she walks up the short wooden porch to the front door anyway. It seems like a halfway point—a way to ease into what is to come. She taps lightly on the door. There is no answer, so she turns the knob and enters the large empty living room. From there she can see half the kitchen and hear the clunky clattering of pans but still sees no one.

"Hello?" she calls.

Aunt Patsy lifts her head from under the counter and then, like she has just comprehended who the voice belongs to, stands. Her lips are half-parted, and her brows lift into the blue kerchief that covers her baldness. She has been done with chemo for three weeks now. Zoe wonders how long before the hair grows back, but she can't ask. She can't even notice. She pretends that Aunt Patsy's eyes aren't hollow, that her wrists aren't thin. Like she is still just the same old Aunt Patsy she always was. Maybe she is. They are all good at pretending.

Aunt Patsy wipes her hands over and over again on her apron when there is nothing on them. "Zoe?" she says. "Zoe." She smiles and comes around the counter with her arms outstretched. "I didn't know—"

Zoe kisses her cheek. "Grandma said I wasn't coming?"

Aunt Patsy nods and glances out the kitchen window that looks out on the back patio. "Oh, yes," she hushes.

"Is it okay? With you?"

Aunt Patsy frowns and blows air out the sides of her mouth, as she draws Zoe into the kitchen. "Everyone is welcome in *my* house, and anyone who gets their knickers in a knot over that will just have to go plant them else-where! You hear?"

"I hear," Zoe says. But she doesn't really. She is fond of Aunt Patsy, but a welcome from her isn't enough.

"Now let's go outside and say hello."

Zoe is still not ready, and she steps away from the door. She asks to borrow some gift wrap for Kyle's present first. Aunt Patsy leads her down the narrow hall, pulls some wrap from a shelf in the closet, and leaves the supplies spread out on a lower bunk in Wain and Kyle's room so Zoe can complete the job. "Hurry now," she says. "Kyle will be happy to see you."

"And Mama? Is she here?"

Aunt Patsy nods but doesn't say anything about Mama being happy to see Zoe. Just a silent nod and she leaves, maybe afraid to get started on any talk of Mama at all on a day that is supposed to be happy for Kyle. *Aunt Patsy has priorities,* Zoe thinks, and she is glad Kyle lives here.

The room is tiny but neat. Every square foot is filled with the orderly storage of boy things. She wonders at the space Wain had to give up in order to squeeze in Kyle—the space in his room, and the space in his life. Some people are able to squeeze, to mold around another life like it has always been there.

Wain is just a year older than Kyle, so their interests are similar. It is a good match, she thinks. Kyle belongs here. She knows Kyle's underwear is always clean. He goes for checkups to the dentist. He has to be in bed by nine on a weeknight. He is missed if he is home late from school and scolded if he causes needless worry. A world revolves with an orderly rhythm and he helps make it happen. A rhythm that she has never known, but surely Grandma thinks otherwise. Grandma imagines it in her mind. They all do. Appearances can be deceiving. A new dress from Kmart for Christmas day can make it all seem so together and right. Appearances. If Mama is here today, will it be a new dress, or easy laughter, or long pants to cover her withering legs that will make it seem that everything is right and Zoe is all wrong? Will her shaking hands or faulty steps be shrugged off with an explanation of little sleep, or a touch of the flu, or whatever else that will make Mama seem right?

Zoe finishes wrapping the awkwardly shaped package, and with nothing else to delay her, she walks down the hallway to the sliding glass door and steps out to the patio to get it over with. She is suddenly overwhelmed with the need to see Kyle. She needs to see his eyes and make sure they haven't changed. She needs to hold him, to rub his head, to soak in the love he is full up with.

She needs some of that before she sees Mama.

TWENTY-TWO

She stares out at the green. It rolls like eternity, an area too big for her voice to penetrate. Too big to whisper, *Come here.* Too big to reach out and gather him to her. Just to her, without the world scrambling in the way. And would he come? Would he be afraid because he knows she loves him and she hates him? She hates him for leaving her. Alone. After everything she did. How could he leave her? She wants to look into his clear, blue, watery eyes that are just like Mama's and ask . . . *why?* And then she wants to slap him. Slap him a hundred times across his beautiful face, and then kiss his tears away and beg forgiveness. Because she loves him. She mostly loves him.

He plays in the five-foot Doughboy pool Uncle Clint set up at the beginning of summer. Wain, too. Their laughter and hoots jump across the hot afternoon air. And the hooligans. The five hooligans Grandma is surely frowning over. But Zoe can't see her face. She is far out in the green expanse, planted at a round table in the shade of an orange-striped umbrella. Her eyes move from Grandma's stiff gray hair to the head next to her. Blond, freshly curled hair is pulled back into a clip.

Mama.

Mama wears a long navy cotton skirt and a blousy red and white top that makes her look cheerful and patriotic. It lifts Zoe. The effort. But she knows about appearances. It settles her, whispers to her, *Don't be fooled, not again.* But it wouldn't take much, she knows, perhaps just a hand cupped tenderly under her chin. The wanting is still there.

+ * +

Kyle spots her. Silhouetted against a hot, silky-white sky, he waves. His arm cuts across the blinding backdrop, back and forth, back and forth, filled with wet, splashing, eleven-year-old freedom.

"Zoe . . . ," his voice calls, but it rolls through the air like a fog, slowly fingering its way to her ears in a blurry echo because, with the waving of his arms, heads turn, and across the distance of grass and betrayal, she is looking eye to eye with Grandma—Grandma turning heavy shoulders, a stiff neck, her jaw cutting the air. Looking. Looking just long enough so Zoe knows. She saw her. And then she turns back, as big and unmoving as the Doughboy pool.

And then Mama, last of all, because sound and movement are curdled for her, and she finally awakens with the knowledge who the turned heads are for, and she turns, too. She stands, her hand balancing a glass that even Aunt Patsy and Uncle Clint can't seem to deny. She lifts her hand, but Grandma grabs her arm and pulls her back into her seat with something urgent that must be said right at that moment. Was it a wave? Was Mama going to wave? But just as quickly, Mama has forgotten her, tucked Zoe back into her sleepy dark memory, and Zoe is staring once again at the back of her head. She wonders, a slow uncurling thought . . . *Did Grandma lie about Mama crying for me? Was that only what Grandma hoped for?*

The knowing crawls up her back, stiffens her. Mama didn't cry.

"Zoe! You came!" And Kyle is upon her, his hair wet, pressing upon her breast, and she doesn't care that he is soaking her crisp ironed clothes she wanted Grandma to see. She holds him, letting the wet glue them together, pressing her lips against dripping cords of hair. Closing her eyes and drinking in the cool and the touch of arms wrapped around her waist.

"Of course, Kiteman. Where else would I be on your birthday?" she says. He pulls away, glancing over his shoulder to his friends, who are calling him back to the pool.

"It's just that . . ." He hesitates. She sees a too-old crease surround his eyes, and the light blue grows dark. "Is it true you left? You left Mama . . . *alone?*"

And then she wants to slap him. Shake him. She wants

to clutch her stomach and squeeze away the hollow his worried eyes have carved in her.

"I had to, Kiteman" is all she can say.

His voice is hoarse, barely a whisper. "Is she going to be okay?"

"I don't know."

He looks down like he is tossing away the thought and then lifts his gaze to her again. "You okay?" he asks.

And all is forgiven for the share of worry that is for her. She ruffles his hair and says, "Go! Stop being such a drudge! Your friends are calling you." His smile returns, and he runs back to the games and worries of being dunked. It is all he has ever known. To move on, because Zoe has made it so. For him. She rubs it out of his hair, out of his life, because she can.

The laughter and splashing resume with a dash and a jump, pushing her back into the world she came from. Alone. The dampness at her breast fades to dryness, and in seconds, Kyle's touch is gone. She smooths out the wrinkles left across her crisp white cotton blouse and sees she forgot to do her nails. Shit. She forgot to do her nails. A wrinkled blouse, ragged nails, and alone.

She looks back at the house, but Aunt Patsy has gone inside. Uncle Clint, his neighbor Odell, and Aunt Patsy's older brother Evan, hover over a barbecue near the storage shed. Evan's wife, Norma, is clucking and playing lifeguard near the pool. And then there are the disapproving backs of Grandma and Mama ready to swallow her up.

"Hello!"

She turns. Out of nowhere, Quentin Hale has descended like an angel to save her from a lawn that pins her to its middle.

"Hello," she says. His ponytail is a full six inches longer than the last time she saw him. A mere nub before, it is now long enough to swing right into Grandma's disapproval. It warms Zoe. Wrinkles have grown out from his eyes, and stubble on his chin glistens in the sun.

"Been a while," he says. She is thankful for his presence, but his voice chills her. It is forever stamped with the nauseating scent of sweet mixed bouquets, carnations and amaryllis wilting in afternoon heat, forever married with the sound of whimpers and echoes and a spade turning over soil. His voice, genuine, warm, but now tainted by a day he had nothing to do with, except for the exchange of a few words.

"Yeah," she says. "Two years, almost. Not since . . ." She doesn't finish.

He nods. "Yeah. Not since." He takes her cue, and she is more grateful now than she has been in the last two years that he is the one who preached at Daddy's funeral. Grandma had howled. "He ain't nothin but a pot-smokin' hippie. Never even seen this side of a seminary. What will folks think? It ain't decent." But Mama had nodded approval.

Daddy had always liked Quentin. Said he was the real deal. And Mama couldn't be swayed. Aunt Patsy's baby brother would see Daddy off to the Great Beyond. "If that's where he's going," Grandma grumbled.

Zoe looks into Quentin's face. She reads it, or tries. She doesn't know about real deals, but if a face can be true, Quentin's is. He may not be a real preacher with a fancy seminary degree or proper pastor clothes, but he is real enough that Ruby First Baptist hired him on as an assistant pastor. He lives in a tiny travel trailer in the parking lot and serves as a pastor on call. He was on call the night they found Daddy.

"You're lookin' good, Zoe. Life treatin' you well?"

Her fingers curl into a fist to hide her nails. "Well, enough," she says. The words sound whiny, and she tries to lighten them with a smile that comes too late.

"Considering?"

"What do you mean?"

"You've had a hard time of it, is all. Lots of growing up for your years."

There has been no growing up, she thinks. "I've always been grown up."

He nods. "Yeah. Guess you have. But you've done good." Good. The words feel like a warm bath on a cold day. She remembers he was kind with Daddy, too. He said nice things he didn't have to say. Words rolled from his lips and hemmed in her tears as she sat in the first pew. Kind words that wrapped her up warm and hopeful and made her think on the good. But why?

"Two years too late to ask a question, you think?" she asks.

"Nothing's ever too late."

Really. In what world? She looks away and squints at the pool in the distance. She shades her eyes like she is more interested in splashing and boys' belly flops, like her question is an idle thought that is casually slipping out. "You really think he's in heaven—Daddy, that is—or was that just preacher talk for a grieving family? He never went to church, you know, and he died dead drunk. Doesn't sound like heaven material to me. And besides that, he—" And it has all run out and doesn't sound casual at all.

"You just now getting around to critiquing my sermon, Zoe, or you got something else on your mind?"

"Nothing else," she says. *Nothing else except Mama.*

Quentin eases her hand down and swings her gently to face him. "We don't know nothin' about that moment he went to meet his maker, Zoe. Nothin', you hear me? No one was there. I think when we get to heaven there's goin' to be a whole lot of gasps and whoops over who's there and who's not. Lots of surprises. I always think on that poor bastard hangin' up 'side Jesus. One minute a sinner and the next walkin' in Paradise. Bet none of them Pharisees could've guessed it. Yep. A whole lot of surprises, 'cause only the Lord knows the heart of a man. Ain't our job to be second-guessin'.'"

He talked a good talk. She knew at least he believed it, and maybe that was all she needed to hear. Possibility. Someone's possibility. Someone believing in someone else. Quentin believing in Daddy. Daddy who was dead. Daddy who had believed in her. Daddy who talked a good talk, too. *Special, Zoe. Stars, Zoe.* Talk. Only talk and nothing more.

But it was enough. At least, then it had seemed enough.

"Gifts!" Aunt Patsy calls. She unloads armfuls of offerings for Kyle onto the picnic table. "Gifts!" she calls again like she is ringing a bell. Other activities are pushed aside, and feet move, gather up like a magnet slowly toward the patio. Norma relays the call, "Gifts," and claps her hands, and the boys are bounding out of the pool and the sky is a quilted flash of towels and hoots.

Zoe turns obediently with Quentin and moves toward the patio, knowing it will bring her elbow to elbow with days of worry and years of wanting.

She hears the murmurs, the heavy footsteps of Grandma and Mama behind her, muffled, shuffling, a low sound no one else can hear but Zoe. A whisper of sound that says, *Run Zoe, don't look back, Zoe.* She picks up her pace and smiles as she steps onto the patch of concrete that will hold them all for the next thirty minutes.

Zoe holds out her arms to Uncle Clint and then greets

Evan and Odell, and then teases with Wain, and the movement is all so carefully orchestrated, so full and busy, that no one notices the gulf between her and Grandma and Mama. It is amazing, she thinks, how simple appearances can be created—a rush, a smile, a new coat of paint, a slow, calm voice, a hug, a new dress—a resolve to keep out questions and cling to secrets.

The boys crowd at the picnic table; the adults scatter in rickety lawn chairs around them. Zoe stands, leaning against the awning pole, holding her distance from both. Uncle Clint warns them that the barbecue will be ready in twenty minutes, and Aunt Patsy clucks that the barbecue will wait for gifts.

"Zoe, sit here," Norma offers, patting the arm of the chair next to her. "There's plenty of room." But there is an empty chair next to Mama, too. Why didn't Mama pat her chair? Why does someone she barely knows notice she is standing, but Mama does not?

She wants to look at Mama. Glare straight into her hazy, indifferent eyes and spit words into her face, but instead she smiles at Norma and says, "Thanks, but I think I'll stand for a while." And the smoothing over, her forced smile and the appearance of contentment, simmers so hotly inside her she doesn't even see the first few gifts that Kyle opens.

And then a card is opened and a twenty-dollar bill falls to the ground. "It's from Aunt Nadine!" he announces as he snatches it up. Mama smiles. Grandma grunts. *Aunt Nadine, the only one smart enough to escape this misery,* Zoe thinks. So far away, but still remembering Kyle and her on their birthdays. Letting go, but maybe not completely.

Paper flies, and then another box. "This one's from Mama," he says, and Zoe shifts feet, stands up straighter, wondering at the large box, the very large box wrapped so carefully. Mama's shaking hands could never have creased the corners so sharply. Not Mama's shaking, fumbling, never-there hands. The details reach out at her, the ribbon, the card, the little squares of tape that hold it all together so nicely. But Kyle is beyond details and rips away paper, barely reading the card, and beams as he throws stuffing away and lifts a skateboard from the box.

"Yes!" he yells. "This is it! This is the one!" He runs to Mama and throws his arms around her neck. He kisses her cheek, and she nods. Her eyes blink. She pats his back.

And Grandma smiles.

Grandma, watching what she has created, smiles and takes a satisfied drag of her cigarette and blows the smoke over her shoulder. "And don't forget the paperwork in the box, Kyle. Them wheels come with a guarantee. Your mama got you the best."

Kyle spins the wheels and ignores the guarantee. The wheels whir a smooth, buttery buzz that saw right into Zoe's bones. "Can I go try it on the front drive?" he asks.

But there is still one present. Zoe's present.

"One more gift," Aunt Patsy says. "Then you can go."

Kyle gives the wheels one more spin and then sets it aside. *Buzz.* The wheels spin. He rips open the awkwardly shaped package. *Buzz.* Zoe sees the details, the crumpled corners, the gaps, and the ribbon that doesn't match. *Buzz . . . run, Zoe . . . hide, Zoe . . . you are nothing, Zoe.*

But it is the Dragonslayer. The Dragonslayer *1000.* For her Kiteman. She stands her ground and forces a faint smile to cover her needy expectation. She works this leg, that arm, to hold them just right to show she is confident because she knows. More than anyone, she knows.

The kite is revealed. It shimmers, its green more brilliant than a hummingbird's throat. Its carefully sewn flaps begging the wind. Its reel made to whir more loudly than a thousand spinning wheels. Norma *oohs.* Uncle Clint and Evan reach out to touch. Quentin nods approval.

But Kyle. It is a glance shorter than a breath—a sideways glance to Wain and a smile that comes a blink too late—that tells Zoe.

She doesn't know.

And even as she hugs Kyle and says "you're welcome," she knows he is not her Kiteman. He is not four years old anymore, he is eleven, for God's sake. Eleven, and he has moved on to skateboards. He moved on. And you didn't know, you stupid shit, *you didn't know.*

But Grandma did.

TWENTY-THREE

Wind blows warm.

Good-byes circle around on a dust cloud and come back again.

"Good-bye."

"Night."

Iridescent wings bat the porch light. Chirps jump across quiet. The sky splits wide with black and silver. Kyle's day. Kyle's evening. All Kyle's. As it should be.

Car doors slam. Quentin gone. Evan and Norma. Gone. An evening. Gone.

Uncle Clint in the doorway. Aunt Patsy on the bottom step. Kyle kissing Grandma's cheek. The wind swirling. The chirps gathering. And Mama still inside. In the bathroom. Zoe knows. Not to pee. A pill-popping break. You can drink less if you chase it with a pill. It doesn't matter what kind. A pain pill. A Valium. Mama has them all. All prescription so it's okay. Okay. Everything is fucking okay. The whole day has been fucking okay. And no one has asked. Not Mama.

Four days she has been alone. But it is not about Zoe. It never has been. Four. But Mama leaves for the rest room to take care of her needs, but never pauses to check on Zoe's. Not a single pause to see if Zoe has eaten, if she has slept, if she has breathed.

And now Kyle is kissing Zoe's cheek. Holding her. And the day that wasn't swells inside her. It swells with its nothingness, and Kyle is running back up the porch steps.

Gone.

"Night," Aunt Patsy says. "Thanks for helping with the dishes," she says. "Thanks for coming," she says. And though Uncle Clint still fills the doorway, the trailer door wedged open, the door on the day is closing, and Zoe is splitting inside with need. It races to her fingertips like electricity and back up again to pinch off her throat. She trembles. It squeezes her spine. Invisible. The door is closing. *You ain't hardly family at all.*

"Night," she says as Mama stumbles back through the door. "Night," she says again as the warm breeze lifts the hair at her neck. And only a sliver of the day is left open when she comes eye to eye with Mama slurring her way down the steps, eye to eye with Grandma grabbing Mama's arm, and the need pulls at her chest, pulls at her shoulder, pulls at the purse resting against her hip, and Zoe shakes it open, before she knows it, she is shaking her purse open so keys rattle. She pulls out her lighter and then a cigarette. The flame ignites with a single strike, and she holds it to the shaking end of the cigarette. She pulls hard. Slowly. She breathes in deeply and exhales. Her smoky breaths stop the good-byes. She lowers her hand to her side, fingers of smoke weaving around her. She tries to hold it easily, but her hand shakes, like all the need and trembling is pouring out through one little cigarette. But it doesn't matter. Every eye is on her. Before the door closes. Every eye looks.

"Zoe?" Uncle Clint says.

Aunt Patsy stares, her mouth open and silent.

Grandma's lips pull tight.

"Sugar," Mama says. Clarity. Crumpled eyes.

"This?" She waves the cigarette, and forces a smile. "I've been smoking for years. I can't believe you never guessed. But I've decided I'm tired of secrets. No more secrets."

Uncle Clint steps out of the doorway. "But, Zoe—"

She turns. "Night," she says. A corner of control. The evening is over because she has made it so. "Night," she calls over her shoulder.

And the jumble of voices at her back melt with the evening wind and ribbon away to nothing.

She is empty.

Or is it full?

Lightness.

She is full up lightness.

TWENTY-FOUR

"Lorelei," she whispers.

It rolls back to her again and again, like a leaf on a gentle tide. It comes back, wet, sweet, easy, to be whispered again. She wonders at such a little word that begs to be said aloud. Three little syllables that make a song. Complete.

She whispers it again, sends it up like a compass, a beacon, as she navigates aisles with a shopping cart that *clack, clack, clack*s to one side with a jittering wheel.

She stops in the jelly aisle. Rupert's Deluxe Concord is endless black-purple and promises satisfaction or your money back. The twelve-ounce jar mimics cut-glass and costs $3.89. It would look pretty on her hutch. But not $2.40 prettier than the Food Star brand that is a little less purple and a whole lot bigger. She slips the fat Food Star jelly jar into the cart next to a ninety-nine-cent loaf of lighter-than-air bread. Peanut butter is next, and she ignores all the claims and offers on the jars—only the price matters. Food Star wins again.

She passes the milk case and pauses. She looks at the little quart cartons. She imagines a glass of cold milk with a peanut butter sandwich. But she has no glasses. And one more item—even a carton of milk—would be too risky. The damn tampons are taking up half her grocery budget, but those she can't do without. She felt the cramping coming on at work, and only two battered tampons lurk somewhere in the bottom of her purse. Four fifty-nine for one stupid box. Even for the Food Star brand. She passes on the milk and picks up a ninety-nine-cent, two-roll package of toilet paper—on special. God bless Food Star.

She checks out. The $9.96 total is four cents under budget. The rest of her Sunday tips will go toward her transportation fee. The sleazebag was generous again. She is almost beginning to like him, in a gagging kind of way. She drops the four pennies change loosely into her purse. They clink against her hairbrush like a metal ball in a pinball machine, a *clink clink, clink* that harmonizes with the word still playing behind her eyes. *Lorelei.* She gathers the bag of groceries to her arms.

"Pardon?" the cashier says.

"What?" Zoe asks.

"Sorry, I thought you said something,"

Zoe pauses, crawls out of her thoughts . . . and smiles. "Yes, I probably did."

And she leaves, the brown paper bag tucked snugly against her chest.

TWENTY-FIVE

Her fingers glide over the wide arm of the Adirondack chair. The purple enamel is uneven. She feels faint indentations where previous layers had peeled, were sanded, and then were painted again. Season by season. A bit of yellow peeks out here, a bit of orange there, but it is mostly purple now, smooth, cool purple. She leans back, closes her eyes, swims in the sounds of Opal's garden. For the first time she feels the teetering edge of autumn. A smell. A chill. The long glint of sun that seems more copper than gold. A difference that is hard to name when it is only just coming on. But it is there. And then, she thinks, it is not. It is once again the last days of summer, her back damp against the slats of wood. Summer, autumn. Autumn, summer.

It's a dance, she thinks. This letting go.

Coming. Going.

Back and forth.

This passing of one season to the next.

How long does it last? But she has never had time to

think about it before. She has never had time to sit in a purple Adirondack chair in the shade of a drooping elm and notice. She doesn't know how long this holding on and letting go lasts.

"Here we are," Opal calls across the yard. She carries a tray. Zoe sits up. It is awkward being served, a role she is not used to. She only came to the garden to explore, a time to wind down after tennis practice and see what lay behind the city of bird feeders. She followed the short path of broken flagstone to the canopy of elms with two purple Adirondacks resting beneath them. It looked like a shady hideaway and the thought made her smile—maybe it should be called Opal's Lorelei Hideout. Opal had come bustling through with a small basket draping her arm, and when she saw Zoe, she squealed and said, "Perfect! Perfect! Sit! I'll be right back! Sit, now! I knew this would happen!" And she hurried to the house. The words sounded like orders, but the tone was joy.

Zoe has been waiting for twenty minutes now—maybe more—but she doesn't mind. The yard, the hideaway, is another world. Slow, apart, an atmosphere all its own. No grass grows below the trees, only a scattering of silver-tipped leaves at her feet. Thin shafts of light break through in half a dozen places, freezing particles of dust in their beams. Gravity doesn't exist in Opal's Lorelei Hideout.

Now Opal comes, full-faced with a smile and wrinkles, and Zoe notices the limp, an ever-so-slight heaviness to the right leg. *I should get up,* she thinks, but she stays. She is like a frozen particle, caught in Opal's beam.

"This is it," Opal says, setting the tray on a slatted table between them. "Last of the season! No more blackberry tea till next summer. I must've picked the last berry just as you walked up—just enough for two glasses. Fate, I think. You believe in fate, Zoe?"

She hands Zoe a droplet-covered glass filled with ice cubes and lavender tea.

"I don't know," Zoe answers. She is not even sure what fate is.

Opal lifts the other glass, and Zoe thinks Opal is lifting possibility as much as tea. She has come to read eyes, too— at least Opal's—and they say as much as her words.

Zoe takes a sip. "It's very good," she says, and means it. She takes another sip. It is fragrant and light and delicately sweet, nothing like the tea at Murray's. She settles back in the Adirondack and rests the glass on the wide arm. "What's fate to you, Opal?" she asks.

Opal leans back, too. "Oh, lots of things. Lots and lots of things all pushed up against each other that make something else happen. So much pushing it just can't happen any other way—unless you push back to make it not."

"Not?"

"Not happen."

"Oh," Zoe says, but the sense of it is floating in and out of her reach, like a season deciding to come or not come.

They sit, enjoying the quiet, the tea, the purple Adirondacks curved just right to their backs, Zoe watching Opal cock her head to the side now and again when a bird takes up a song. Zoe's eyes travel down the arm of the chair to Opal's short leg and thick-soled shoe. What things pushed up against each other to make that happen? She watches Opal absently rubbing her thigh.

"Your leg bother you much?" Zoe asks, and then thinks it was a rude question. Rude to notice. A short leg. She should have looked away.

But Opal rolls right over the rudeness, eager to answer. "Just these later years now and again. Never bothered me before. I think it's arthritis settling into the break. Heard that happens."

"You broke your leg?"

"Oh sure, that's what made it shorter in the first place. It broke in just the right—well, just the wrong place for an eight-year-old. It still grew after that, but not near as much as the other."

"How did it happen?"

"I didn't move fast enough or jump high enough to please my pap. Don't remember the why of it so much as the how. He had a temper shorter than Count Basil's tail and broke a two-by-four across my thigh. My ma joked later that if he had hit it over my head I would have been just fine. I did have a way about me, I suppose."

"Your mother joked about it?"

Opal snorts and waves her hand like she is swatting at a fly. "Oh, years later. By then she had killed the old man, so it seemed all right to do."

Zoe cannot find graceful words to respond, and the ones on the edge of her lips won't do. It is too bizarre. Not so much the killing but how Opal speaks of it. Like she is speaking of someone else. Like she is so detached she can still be happy. How can she drink tea and smile at another birdsong in the same breath as the telling of her mother killing her father?

Opal sips more tea and shakes her head. "Seems like five lifetimes ago. I hardly think of it anymore." A faint, dreamy smile crosses her face again, and Zoe wonders how such a memory could bring a smile. Or maybe the smile is having almost forgotten? Or just that it doesn't matter so much anymore? Could something like that ever get so distant that it doesn't matter? Or maybe the smile is just that she survived it? Is that it? Surviving? But Opal seems like she is doing much more than surviving. She seems to squeeze the most from every moment. Zoe thinks of Opal's squeal at finding her in the garden and then hurrying away to make the tea. Every moment is *the* moment for Opal. Like she can't let a single one get past her. Or maybe all these moments push out the others. Make up for the others. Push them as distant as five lifetimes.

New moments of Opal's own making.

Zoe picks at an orange-yellow-purple indentation,

seasons and seasons' worth of distant painted-over moments, as far away as Opal needs them to be.

A gentle cooing cuts into her thoughts. "Do you hear that?" Zoe asks. She cocks her head to the side as she has seen Opal do. "Mourning doves. I'm sure it's mourning doves."

Opal cocks her head to the side, too, alert, but the cooing has stopped. "They're shy," she says. "Won't come near the feeders with the other birds, but sometimes early I will see them there. Gentlest creatures. And loyal."

"Yes," Zoe agrees. "I know." She and Kyle used to feed them bread crumbs on the walk in front of their house. They came back morning after morning. The doves were the closest thing to pets they ever had.

Zoe drinks down the last of her blackberry tea. "So you think it's the end of the season?" she asks.

"According to my berry bushes. But a few others are hanging on. Still have a few apricots on the tree. Can you believe that? September and still apricots! It's the shade of the mulberry, I suppose."

Kyle loves apricots, Zoe thinks. Mr. Henderson always brings over bags full of them from his tree, but it is finished up by the beginning of August. Kyle probably hasn't had an apricot since then. Neither has she.

And Mama. Mama loves apricots, too.

"Then I guess according to your apricots it's still summer," Zoe says, and with the passing of a warm breeze across her arms, she thinks it must be true.

TWENTY-SIX

Filthy money, Murray calls it.

    Dirty from so many germy hands touching it.

    But as she slides soft, wrinkled bills—

        thirty-four singles,

two fives,

      and one,

           two,

                three,

     four

        quarters—

across the counter, the echoes of dozens of yes ma'ams, yes
sirs, my pleasure ma'am, groaning arches, smiles on cue,
extra mayo, no mayo, orders that beg to be confused but
aren't, anything elses, and come back agains . . . they follow
the money like ghosts, make it more than money, and she
can't describe it as dirty because

                as she lets go,

                    it feels amazingly clean.

"Forty-five," the clerk says. "Here's your receipt. We'll send a copy to your coach so he knows you're clear on your transportation fee."

Another bill checked off. Accomplished. Done. Day by day.

It's working.

It was close. After the Food Star groceries, one pack of cigarettes, and a single gallon of gas to top off the fumes she's been driving on for two days, she only has five cents left from her Sunday, Tuesday, and Thursday tips combined. But close is good enough, and the satisfaction of a paid bill spreads over her like new paint on a dingy wall. No excuses. No talk. Just done.

And no crawling back.

"Something else?" the clerk asks.

Zoe realizes she has used the clerk's counter and time to wade through her thoughts while a line grows behind her. "No, nothing," she says. Her victory is her own, solitary and unnoticed.

She starts to turn away and feels each elbow being caught up.

"So when were you going to tell us?"

"You got a secret to share?"

Reid pulls on one side. Carly on the other. Monica and Jorge squeeze close by. Their attention doesn't lift Zoe. They know. It cuts her open. Her world is not theirs. It never has been. A brittle shade separates them—or did. But now the dirty secrets of her life are bared, and embarrassment laps in. How did they find out? *Please, not Mama. I hope they didn't talk to Mama.* She is stupid. Of course they would call eventually. Now appearances, even thin ones, are gone.

"What I want to know is how you can afford it."

"It's called a job, Monica," Jorge says.

"Shut up, shit-for-brains. I wasn't asking you. Besides, I have a job, and I could never afford an apartment."

"It's not an apartment," Zoe says.

"Well, what is it then? A house?" Jorge asks.

"I—"

Reid stops and spins her to face him. "Did you rent a whole fucking house?"

Carly breaks in. "No. She bought it. She bought a whole house, you idiot. Would you let her talk!"

"It's a room," Zoe says, "on Lorelei Street." Her words are like a stamp. A final approval. Or maybe more like full disclosure. No going back.

"Where's that?"

They guide her to the parking lot, and during the ten minutes they have before the bell rings, they share a smoke between cars while she answers their questions. "It's off of Carmichael about six blocks from the diner."

"How big is it?" Carly asks.

"I told you. It's a room. That's all. And a bathroom. And sort of a kitchen in one corner. A sink, a hot plate, and a refrigerator." She leans against the car that hides them and

166

takes the shared cigarette from Reid's fingers. Their enthusiasm cinches her up, edges away the embarrassment. She squints and wants to have some fun. She inhales and blows a long dramatic trail out. Effect for Reid. Pause. Timing. It all matters. "Came with a dog, too. I share the room with a bulldog. A big, fat-ass bulldog."

"No way!" Reid says. She knows he is more impressed with her delivery than the dog. Monica and Carly both laugh and scream "What?" at the same time. Jorge maintains control. He is not interested in the dog. "What about a Jacuzzi?" he asks.

Zoe and Monica exchange a look. The question goes unanswered. The warning bell rings, Zoe passes the cigarette to Carly for a last puff, and they walk to class. At the 200 wing the group splits—Zoe goes with Carly, and Reid, Monica, and Jorge head off in another direction.

"How'd you find out?" Zoe asks. "You called the house?"

"Yeah," Carly answers.

Zoe feels a stiffening to her cheeks. A bracing to keep the turn of her lips and the tilt of her chin just so. "So you talked to my mom," she says.

"No. I talked to your grandma. She's the one who answered."

Grandma? Her room was revealed by Grandma? A corner is stolen. A patchwork pillow. A star. A bulldog. A fingerprint smudge. *Damn you, Zoe. Why didn't you tell them first?* The careful bracing is gone. "What did she say?"

"Just that you moved out. Gave me the address and then said something about secrets that I didn't get."

Secrets.

Carly's voice becomes careful. Delicate. "She . . . sounded a little . . . funny. Just said you moved out because you were tired of secrets. Kind of leaned heavy on that word. What'd she mean?"

She meant for you to tell me, that's what she meant, Zoe thinks. *She wanted to steal a piece of my day. My life. Make her thoughts my thoughts. To throw my words back in my face. She meant to control me without ever speaking to me.* But Zoe says none of those things to Carly.

"I don't know," she answers in a voice that even Reid would have believed.

TWENTY-SEVEN

Zoe stares at the whiteboard, watches Mr. Crain scrawl numbers across it, but the white, the glare, the white that seems to wrap around her and hold her, white that squeezes her, glimmers, white that shines like water, like porcelain,
the white is all she sees.

Shimmering white that holds water and secrets. Grandma knows. She tosses the word *secret* to Carly, knowing she will toss it to Zoe, like a key that will let Grandma in. Let Grandma control her. The porcelain white that she sees every day of her life. Mr. Crain dissolves away. She only sees a glimmering white tub, and her mind travels around and through every shiny inch of it.

Is it possible for a grown man to drown in sixteen inches of water? To be so drunk that when he slips beneath the surface he can't find his way up again, so that up mixes with down, dry mixes with wet, air mixes with liquid, until all is blackness and he is gone? Was it possible for Daddy to be so stinking drunk he could slide beneath the water and not know it? To breathe in the warm, gray water and think it is air? Not even convulse automatically upward for a breath? Can anyone be that drunk? The investigators said maybe, yes, probably, and then they saw that the overflow was clogged. A few extra inches in the tub. How could that make a difference? Maybe. It could. But then again. But Grandma hollered and wailed, and the insurance company settled. A few extra inches and Daddy being drunk didn't matter anymore. He drowned in their tub because of a clogged overflow. But there was more they didn't know. Would never know. Only she, Grandma, and Mama knew.

They knew more about that night he drank himself into oblivion in a tub full of water. Some secrets were worth money. Some secrets were worth silence. And now Grandma throws it in her face. The night Daddy died and the bath he never should have taken. The suspicion. The night and the wondering that can never be answered because Daddy is gone. The wondering that eats. Daddy is gone because he couldn't face staying.

The official story is it was an accident. The investigators said so. The insurance company said so. Grandma said so. It probably was. But Mama never said a word. She just cried. The secret was not mentioned. Couldn't be mentioned.

Daddy never took baths.

+ + +

The bell rings, and words and numbers appear on the whiteboard. Numbers that have no place in her secret white world. Zoe closes her book. She doesn't write down the homework assignment. It doesn't seem to matter.

Two points for Grandma.

TWENTY-EIGHT

Reid holds her arm. "Well? Tonight, okay?"

"Reid, I'm going to be late!"

He holds on, waiting for an answer. She managed to maneuver away at lunch. She can pull distractions from thin air. But Reid has caught on. He holds her so distractions can't slip in, not even being late to class.

"You mean all of you?" Zoe asks. She doesn't have to emphasize the "all," she knows he will catch it. Words and delivery are his life.

Reid squints. "Yeah." He pauses, nods. "All of us."

She knows that may not have been his plan. Not *all* of them. But so what. Life sucks. Get over it. "Sure," she says. "Nine or so. I gotta—"

The bell rings.

"—go." *Shit.* She is only three steps from Mrs. Garrett's door. Three lousy steps, but it might as well be three miles. She slips in the door, her breath tucked in. The room is seated. Silent. Mrs. Garrett does not look up from her lectern; her eyes are fixed on the folder she is fingering, penciling with marks. Two seconds. Three. It is a breath, a pause, a big fat nothing, before she is in her seat. She barely slices the silence. So what?

Mrs. Garrett looks up, stares at the bug Zoe has become. She sweeps her eyes across Zoe, slowly, like the effort barely interests her. *It's three fucking seconds. Three.* But it's more than that. Zoe knows. More than three seconds, more than the word *fuck* spoken aloud in a classroom on the first day of school, more than a mispronounced name.

It's being. Wanting to be. More than. Less than. Something. Anything. She can feel it. It pushes against her ribs; it is heavy in her stomach. She holds it in. Pins it away to a secret part of her soul. Mrs. Garrett thinks Zoe will break. In what reality? She has said it before. She tells herself again. *Mrs. Garrett is a cakewalk.* She opens her book and prepares to enter her invisible world for the next hour. She is getting used to it. Cake. Walk. I. Am. Not. A.

Bug.

A paper is returned at the end of class.

Zoe barely glances at the grade scrawled across the top before she slides it into her notebook. She can't let on that it matters. It's all about maneuvers. Her face is blank. But the B-minus pushes at the corner of her mouth. She is making it. Zoe Beth Buckman. Zoe, who can hold it in. Zoe, fourth on the tennis team and moving up. Zoe, who pays her bills on time. Zoe, a B student. Zoe, having friends over to her room. Her own room at 373 Lorelei Street. The room that is working. Cakewalk. Yeah.

TWENTY-NINE

The usual afternoon breezes vanish. Heat wells in layers, one pressing on another. The black asphalt surrounding trailer 10A shimmers like tar, like the late summer heat has melted it back into ooze. Zoe is melting, too. But still, she would rather be on the courts getting in more practice than sitting in an air-conditioned trailer with Mr. K. She has a match today. Practice matters.

The ramp pings and warps as she walks up, but this time she doesn't care if he knows she is coming. It is her third meeting, and she understands Mr. K now. She knows his game. Waitressing has been good for her in that respect at least. If you hope to make decent tips, you have to know what people want. Not just food. Food is nothing. It's more than that. It's when to be quiet, when to be chatty, when to smile, when to fade away. Mr. K wants chat. She can give him that without revealing a thing, and in return she might get an early release from this tin prison. Leaving early will mean catching the bus to the match, and that means saving gas. Like practice, gas matters. It all works together to keep the room.

The door swings and barely cool air hits her face. It smells of dusty carpet, stale popcorn, and body odors that should be reserved for second grade. *Thank you, Mr. K*, but in her next cool breath she knows it is not Mr. K who must be thanked.

"Come in. Here. Come." A twitchy, hawk-nosed man motions to where she sat last week. She doesn't move. He is nervous. Sweaty. Why? He swings his angled body toward her and holds out his hand. *Cripes! Who is this geek?* "Mr. Beltzer. I'm filling in for Mr. Kowalashosky. From the district office."

She doesn't like him. His eyes move too fast. His skin is waxy and colorless. And he does strange things with his upper lip. It crinkles and smacks like something is wedged in his front tooth. This was not part of the deal. Suddenly she wants Mr. K. She wants his calmness, his rounded belly, his slow, smooth movements. Suddenly she thinks she did want to talk to Mr. K after all. She wanted him to listen. She wanted to think thoughts aloud and have his quiet way make sense of it all.

"Where's Mr. K?" she asks.

"Out." He twitches, smacks, and sits down. "Looks to be a while. He's in the hospital, something to do with his back." He shuffles through papers, avoiding Zoe's stare. "Traction, I think."

Traction. Zoe sits. She thinks of Mr. K's rounded belly, tight against his white shirt, pulling, pulling against his back, pulling to slide out a vertebra, and then one thing, one small thing finally does it. Maybe a jelly bean. Did one little jelly bean make everything tumble out of line? Make everything fall apart? Even Mr. K, who listens and thinks and knows, could not have known one little jelly bean could make everything come undone. One little jelly bean and his spine careers out of control like a car wreck.

"It will take me just a few minutes," Mr. Beltzer says as he shuffles through a file. "I need to familiarize myself with a few things." He looks up and does the crinkle and smack with his upper lip. "And then we'll talk, all right?"

Zoe wonders if a piece of lettuce is stuck between his gum and lip. It could be. She sees it all the time at Murray's. The liver, piled with slimy gum-sucking onions, does it every time. The "lip boogie" they call it. She could make him smile to find out, say something outrageous to expose his upper gum, but he's not really worth the effort. They won't be talking. She shrugs. "Take your time."

He does. She senses he wishes he could spend the whole hour reading through his files. He twitches, glances. His eyes shift around the room. He gets up twice to adjust the air. What about her makes him uncomfortable?

After fifteen minutes he sets aside the file. There are more twitches, smacks, and eyes that flash past hers, in-a-hurry eyes, don't-speak-to-me eyes, and then finally, comes the

obligatory question. "What would you like to talk about?"
He smacks again, and it cracks through her head like a bat.
Two months ago. Maybe three. Smacks. Giggles. A pinched
breast. A good night. And Mama stumbling through the
door. She can't be sure. She didn't see his face.

But there are so many. Odds are he was one.

"Why don't we both just give it a rest?" she says. "I won't
tell if you won't."

He doesn't answer. He straightens files and smooths his
hand across his mouth like it will straighten out the twitching. "If that's the way you want it," he finally says, and they
spend the remaining forty minutes in silence.

The bell rings and Zoe stands. Mr. Beltzer waves her
back down. "Key Club needs this room for their activities
on Fridays, so starting next week Group will meet on
Wednesdays."

"I'll be sure to spread the word to the rest of the
'Group,'" she says. He doesn't look up.

"I think next time Mrs. Farantino will be filling in, and
hopefully the week after that, Mr. Kowalashosky will be
back. If not, we'll be sure to have someone else here for you."

"Great," she answers. "These sessions have been *so* help-
ful. Thanks, Mr. Belfry."

"Beltzer."

"Right." She stands again, but she can't leave. Yet. "Tell
Mr. K hi for me—and tell him to watch out for those jelly
beans. The innocent little pink ones can be the worst." She

holds his stare. Plays with it. A pause. A long, spacious pause so he feels its weight.

So he knows, she knows.

But as she walks out, her disgust is more for Mama. How could she? How could anything be so important that you would press your lips against waxy, twitching skin? Is there anything Mama wouldn't do for another drink? What happened to Mama? *What happened? That* is the question she would like to ask Mr. Belwhatever. But it's a question she can't ask and will never ask. Because no one knows except Mama and maybe Grandma. And they won't tell. They won't even think of the question. Some things drift down, drift away, where they should be. Drift away because it's better there. That place of no answers.

She grips the doorknob. No room for Zoe. No counselor for Zoe. Next week, Mrs. Farantino. Maybe. She slivers open the door and slips through its crack.

THIRTY

She rushes, but the bus is gone.

They don't wait for anyone, especially dangerous, cursing criminals like her. She hurries to her car to catch up. If she is late to the courts at Gorman High, the coach will assign her to the barely-worth-it matches. He runs a tight ship, he says. Everyone must pull their weight and that includes being on time. She hates his ship analogies. For God's sake, there isn't a boat or a lake within a hundred miles. But the buses move slowly. If she hurries, she can catch up. She'll change clothes in the car at signals. Give some old geezer a thrill. Or maybe change on the long stretch between the refineries and Gorman. It's flat and straight, so a knee and cruise control can take care of the necessities. She aced her match with Lisa Dobson at the last practice. Lisa, who is third on the team—or was. The coach noticed. So did Amy and Kendra, the first and second on the team. And so did Opal, who cheered and waved her flag. She won't be late. Not for this match. She is Zoe Beth Buckman, who makes

Mr. Bel-up-his-ass sweat and tremble, and makes the tight-as-a-ship coach take notice.

She presses on the gas, and the Thunderbird squeals out of the parking lot. She steers with one hand and unbuttons her shirt with the other. The signals cooperate and she is out of Ruby, and then Duborn, in nine minutes. She searches the ribbon of highway ahead for a glimpse of yellow. Nothing. She eases the gas pedal farther to the floor. Today is her day. She can feel it. And she won't be late so Opal can only cheer her on in a lousy doubles-baby-burp match.

Where is the damn bus? The refineries are in sight but not a trace of yellow anywhere. How could they have gotten so far so fast? She pushes the speedometer to seventy-five and rummages through her sports bag on the seat beside her, pulling out her team T-shirt. She holds the steering wheel with her knee as she slips off her blouse. Today's match fills her head. Something to celebrate when she has friends over tonight. The thought clutches her stomach with its newness. A celebration at her own place without worry of Mama slurring into the middle of it all. She will be lighter. Lighter than she has ever been. But the lightness always comes paired with guilt. Mama is alone.

"I can't think about you." She shoves thoughts of Mama aside before they can steal her concentration. She passes the last row of trailers at Sunset Gardens and still no sign of the bus. Did they leave early? She is a hair short of eighty, and the buses go a slow fifty miles per hour. And then she sees it, a boxy glimpse of yellow just as the highway begins to curve. She eases on the gas and heaves a breath she didn't know she was holding, but in the same breath another color flashes her eyes. Red. Flashing red in her rearview mirror, and in an instant her chest seems to burst upward through her throat. "Shit!" The explosion travels back down to her toes. "Shit!" She lets up on the gas. "You *stupid, stupid,* shit!"

Brakes.

Shaking feet.

Rubbery fingers.

They swirl together in hot splinters as she pulls off the road onto the graveled shoulder. The vacuum of the car vibrates and she sits, frozen. Seconds or hours blend together and then knuckles rap against her window and she remembers. Roll window down, show license, don't argue. She cranks the window down and looks up at the trooper, the broad rim of his hat shading his face.

"That ain't going to win any points with me, young lady. Now, why don't you cover it up and then give me your license."

She didn't think it could get worse, but it does. The small amount of adrenaline left in her body shoots out in needles across her chest. "Oh, my God—" She grabs at the T-shirt on the seat next to her. "I—" She pulls it over her head. "I was changing."

"Changing while you drive?" He shakes his head. "License. Now."

She fumbles through tissues, brushes, and hair clips for her wallet and holds it out for him, embarrassed at her shaking hands.

"Out of the wallet, please."

Her fingers are hot and clumsy as she picks and pulls and finally frees the license from its sticky vinyl pocket. She glances ahead. The yellow bus is out of sight.

"Zoe Beth Buckman, huh?"

"Yes, sir." Her voice trembles.

"You ain't going to start crying now, are you? Because that don't win any points with me neither."

"No, sir." *Pull it together.* And then a sliver of light hits her. The rumble of his voice. The crease of his cheeks. *Thank you, miss. You have a good day, too.* "Eggs over easy. Tabasco. Double order of bacon. Extra crisp. Right?"

He pauses, his head tilts slightly to the left and then back again. "You know how fast you were going, Zoe?"

What does she say? What is the right answer? He is obviously not impressed with her good memory. If she lies will she piss him off more? If she tells the truth will she fry her own butt? There has to be a best answer, a fast answer that will get her back on the road behind the bus, but she doesn't know what it is. She wishes she had talked to Carly. After Carly's two speeding tickets, she would at least know what *not* to say.

"Too fast?" she says. Good. Noncommittal. She can always backtrack.

"You got it. Eighty in a fifty-five zone." He pushes his hat back on his head so light slashes across his face and the creases deepen. He leans down, into her window. "And I got more bad news for you. Don't appear you've got a current registration, leastways by the validation sticker on your window. You're two months out. You got some newer stuff tucked in your glove box for me?"

She doesn't bother to look. She knows Mama. The precious sticker lies in a mountain of untouched mail on a kitchen counter in a house that is no longer a house. She leans her head back against the rest and closes her eyes. It's over. "No," she answers. "Nothing newer."

He is silent, and Zoe opens her eyes. He shifts his weight and leans in further. "Well, looks like I've got me a problem then, Zoe. By law I need to haul you in for an overnight stay at the county hotel—that one with the vertical bars? Can't just write you a speeding ticket and ignore the expired registration. Know what I mean? You've done double-duty."

Her breath is gone. This makes Carly's tickets look like a slap on the hands. Jail. How can this be happening to her?

"I'd hate to see you in jail, though. I got a daughter near-about your age. She's a good girl, but she messes up now and then. That's what I'd like to think about you, Zoe. That you're a good girl, law-abiding, and just this once that pedal got away from you. And now that it's been brought to your attention, you'd never let it happen again. That's what I'd like to think. You suppose I'd be right in that line of thinking?"

"Yes, sir. Very right. Very, very right."

"Good. That's what I was hoping to hear. I think I could let you go with a warning then—on *one* condition. You get yourself down to the county tax office first thing Monday and take care of that registration."

"I have school Monday."

"They're open till five. You go to school all day?"

"No, sir. Just till two-thirty."

"Then that'll give you plenty of time to drive real slow and still be there by five."

"Yes, sir. Thank you, sir. But I'm sure that I have it at home anyway. I just need to put it on the window. I'll take care of it. I promise."

"See that you do. And with a good memory like yours, you probably know just what day I'll be coming around for my Philly and fries—and to check for your sticker."

"Tuesday."

"That's right. Now, you be on your way, and if I were you I'd stay off the roads as much as possible until you get that sticker on. The next trooper may not take as kindly to you. You hear what I'm saying?"

"Yes, sir. Thank you, sir. I will." And now she has said "yes, sir" and "thank you" more times in five minutes than she has ever said at Murray's all day.

But it's okay, because she got out of the ticket, has only lost ten minutes, and if she hurries, she can still catch up with the bus.

THIRTY-ONE

Reid won't like it.

But there is nothing she can do about it now. And they're only friends, after all. That's all they've ever been. Maybe it's because there has been no one since him that he thinks it meant more than it did.

"Well, tonight should put an end to that," she whispers. It's a favor, really. He can move on. We all have to move on. She wonders if she should tell the others ahead of time, before Carlos knocks on her door. "No, just wait till he comes." It's not like she planned it. She ran into him in Murray's parking lot when she picked up her paycheck. "It's a free country." If she wants to invite someone to her place, she shouldn't have to feel guilty about it.

"It's my place, after all and—" *God, I'm talking out loud to myself!* She shakes her head. "Reid, you're such a pain." She empties the second grocery bag and checks her watch. Eight-thirty. Another half an hour or so before they come. She splurged. Cigarettes, sodas, chips, salsa, frozen taquitos, and two dozen chocolate cookies from the Food Star bakery. And a tiny votive candle from the clearance bin. It's Friday. Payday. Her very own first company is coming. And she aced her match. More than aced it, she was the star.

The absolute star.

Everyone noticed, not just the coach. She was on like she has never been. She is entitled to celebrate. It's only a few chips. A bit more, maybe. Altogether just thirteen dollars' worth of celebration. Not much, considering. Rent is due next week, but she still has the rest of her paycheck. With her usual tips, she'll have enough. It'll work. Close— but it's working. "Mama should see me now," she whispers. God, she wishes Mama could see her. So what if she has to live on leftover frozen taquitos and chocolate cookies for the next week? It's more than Mama lives on.

She folds the grocery bag and tucks it away in the closet. Time to kill. She turns off the overhead lamp and lights the candle on her hutch. Rings of light bounce off walls and ceiling. Her light. She owns it. Where it goes. When it goes. The room is quiet, so dark, except for her tiny bargain-bin circle of light. Her legs bend, easing her into the chair, and she is sitting with her hands cupped around the candle, relaxed, fingers warmed by the tiny flame, drawn into the glow, glimmer by unbroken glimmer, until she unexpectedly sees Grandma, Kyle, and a lonely night she had long forgotten.

The vanilla scent closes her eyes to the now and takes

her back to the then, pulls her into a downy patched quilt next to Grandma . . . three rings dancing on a ceiling and Grandma cooing first to her and then to Kyle. . . . *Those three rings are us. We're dancing on the ceiling now, aren't we? Having a party all our own and no one else can dance on a ceiling like us.* . . . And Kyle giggles at the nonsense, but Zoe snuggles in closer to Grandma under the covers. Grandma's arm around her, her touch on Zoe's shoulder is like butter on warm bread. It melts in. Fills the holes. Kyle falls into his toddler snores, but she and Grandma watch the circles of light.

Together they stay awake and watch.

"When is Mama coming for us?" she finally asks. But Grandma nestles her in closer and talks about going for doughnuts and hot chocolate in the morning and the fine time they will have. She fills the void of Mama with talk and promises, but Zoe just notices her weathered arms holding her close—her touch, and the scent of clean sheets and vanilla candles that lock up the night to make her safe. And for that night, with Grandma's knobby fingers rubbing close against her arm, she didn't think about Mama anymore.

Zoe returns to her room. To the now. Rubs her arms, remembering Grandma's hands. Dry. Chapped. Working hands. Holding her. Caring.

Trying to make everything right.

A gentle tap at the door startles Zoe. The tap is not from the outer door that leads to the stairs, but the inner door that leads to the rest of the house. A stream of light tumbles into her room as she eases it open, and there is Count Basil, holding a paper bag between his teeth. Opal jumps from the hall, her airy blue caftan billowing around her, and calls, "Surprise!"

She and the Count enter the room. "Go on," she says. "Look inside!" Count Basil drops the bag and plops down by the stone bulldog, already tired by his efforts, but Opal is rubbing her hands together and beaming like a six-year-old. Zoe opens the bag and pulls out a flowing red crushed-velvet robe like a queen might wear. Large rhinestones are sewn across the hem, and white fur edges the collar. It is lined with royal blue satin. Zoe looks at Opal, not sure what it means. "For you!" she says. "Zoe! Queen of the Courts! I went up to the attic as soon as we got home. I hadn't seen it for years, but I knew it was around here somewhere. Never was for me—bought it at a rummage sale—but I knew it was right for someone. They'd come along someday, so I kept it. And today was the someday! I just knew it! Go on! Try it!"

Zoe hesitates. But it is only for fun. And yes, dammit, she is Queen of the Courts! At least for today. She swings it around her shoulders, and Opal squeals. "Yes! I was right! I was right!" Opal bends at the waist in a deep curtsy and rises again, "All hail to Queen Zoe!" She claps her hands like their performance is complete.

Zoe is uncomfortable. It is silliness. The play of children.

Not for someone as old as she, but a smile still escapes her. Opal is crazy and for the moment she is, too—no one will know. She clutches the robe close, lifts her tennis racket from the bed like a scepter, and taps Opal's shoulders.

"You may breathe in my presence," she says in the most royal voice she knows.

Opal smiles back, like Zoe has truly given her a gift. Not the gift of breathing, but something else. It hangs in the air between them, almost touchable, and Zoe turns away.

"You *were* marvelous," Opal says in her soft bird warble.

Zoe takes the robe from her shoulders and tries to fold it back into the neat nondescript ball it once was. "Why do you come, Opal?"

"Oh! There is so much that could happen! I might see you win! And I did! Or I might meet a beau in the bleachers! Or the Count might meet a nice *girl!*" Zoe takes in the way Opal says "girl," drawn out with so much possibility. "Or you might need me to come down and hit a few balls! Opal saves the day! I can see the headlines! Or I might see you win! Oh, I said that already, didn't I? And I did see you win! See?"

Zoe is not sure if the why was answered, but it doesn't seem to matter so much after all, and she is satisfied with Opal's possibilities. But then, the short space of silence tugs a few more words from Opal's lips: "And it's a need."

Zoe looks up. Opal's eyebrows are raised, smoothing the

wrinkles from her eyes. Zoe tries, but she cannot read the faded green flecks in the old woman's eyes, or the timbre of her voice. "Yours . . . or mine?" she asks.

Opal's brows come together. "Does it matter?"

The something is there again, floating between them, and Zoe looks down. She picks at the ivy print of her comforter. "I think I know what you meant," she says.

"Meant?"

"What you said the other day about fate. All those things pushing up against each other so it can't happen any other way."

"Hmm," Opal says.

"I felt that today. That's all. So maybe I do believe in fate. Today was meant to happen. I could feel it in my bones. Do you ever feel that way?"

"All the time, dear. My bones are always speaking to me." She sighs and tucks a stray corkscrew into her turban, looking past Zoe. Creases appear at her eyes and their focus drifts to another world.

Zoe watches Opal's distant concentration and wonders what dreamy thought is passing. Is she flipping through all the moments that have pushed away the past? Is the ache in her short, broken leg pushed aside by the life she has created? Are all those cheerful breezy moments her corner of control, the way the room is for Zoe?

But then just as quickly as the dreamy mood came, it

goes and Opal's eyes sparkle again with focus. Control. She claps her hands. "And my bones are speaking to me now! I have to go—the Count and I have a date on the roof! We're sleeping there tonight. A meteor shower at two, and we won't miss it! You're welcome to join us! Bring a blanket. Just take the attic stairs to the lookout."

"Thanks. But, no. I'm having friends over tonight. We'll just be looking at these stars." She glances at the ceiling.

"Oh," Opal drawls. "Good enough. Come along, Basil," she says and glides out of the room like a billowy cloud with the Count close behind, his stubby rear end wagging. The door closes out the hallway light once again, and her candlelight circle flickers back into its place on her ceiling.

A dog who likes stargazing, Zoe thinks. *Who would have thought?*

THIRTY-TWO

Carly fills the length of the window seat. Monica lies on the bed, bouncing her crossed leg to the beat of "La Bamba" on the jukebox. Reid leans back in the only chair with his feet propped against the bedpost. The room is full in a way Zoe tries to memorize, like a photograph.

It has never been this way. Before the air was always stretched thin, taut, ready to snap. Not from them, but her. Mama might walk in. Would walk in. Talking too loud. Dressed in too little. Hugging too closely. Swaying too much. Too much of everything so Zoe was ready to jump. Explain. Defend. Make sense of Mama. Because she had to. She was still her mama. And she was beautiful. She was gentle. She was more. Once.

But Mama is not coming in. Won't be coming in. Ever. Their relaxation is hers, too. She catches it as it ripples through the room. Tries it out, even breaths, moments that are free of time, clock-watching, and door-watching. It is new, and doesn't quite fit her yet.

She throws her legs over the side of the bed and grabs another Dr Pepper from the refrigerator. "Who was Jorge's hot date?" she asks.

"Melanie Hobson," Monica answers.

"He ditched us for *her?*" Reid asks.

Carly sits up. "He's got a freakin' date on a Friday night, doesn't he?" Carly says. "That's how it's supposed to work, in case you forgot, and it's more than you can say for any of us."

Zoe clears her throat and spreads her royal robe out from her shoulders for another full view. "Excuse me? Are you not out at a friend's very own apartment? A friend who not only won all her tennis matches and is the *official* Queen of the Courts, but also talked herself out of a *speeding ticket* today?"

"You *what?*"

Zoe savors the pitch of Carly's voice. The disbelief. She takes in the way Reid's feet drop to the floor and he leans forward. She loves Monica's attentive twist of her head. And maybe . . . maybe she loves the way she can tell them the whole story and no one will interrupt. No sudden appearances and rushed excuses will take her moment away.

"That's right. Learn from a pro." She tells the story. No one interrupts. Except when she tells about taking her shirt off. Reid makes her tell that part again.

"No way!" he says. But he believes her. She knows. It is Reid playing to her, center stage. Letting her build and make the most of a moment that could have been lost. She is grateful to him for it. She loves him like a brother, and for an instant she wishes Carlos weren't coming. Not for her sake, but for Reid's.

"I bow to the queen," Carly says, getting up. "If I had known that all it took was to go shirtless for those troopers, I would have saved myself a hundred and fifty bucks."

"Three hundred," Reid corrects. "You've had two tickets, but I don't think you've got three hundred worth of anything under your shirt."

Carly throws a small purple pillow across the room at him but misses and hits the bulldog instead.

"Wasn't the shirt anyway," Monica says. "They just didn't want a hundred pounds of mouth in their jail."

"Thanks, Monica," Zoe says. "A hundred and eighteen actually."

Monica shrugs. "There you go."

"Well, I'm taking my fat mouth out for a smoke. Wanna come?" Zoe grabs her cigarettes and lighter from her purse and goes out to the porch. Opal never said she couldn't smoke in the house, but it is her choice. She doesn't want the stale smell of smoke clinging to her walls like it does— What should she call that other place now? It's not home anymore, but it hasn't been a home for years. The other place. She won't have her room smelling like that. No oily, smoke-stained walls. No heavy dreariness to cover her indigo ceiling and stars.

Maybe if Mama had stars . . .

She shoves down the hope like a threadbare rag to the bottom of the trash where useless things belong. Only Reid joins her on the porch. They share a cigarette.

"Where's the landlady?"

"Shhh. Up on the roof."

Reid leans out from the railing, trying to get a look. "She spend a lot of time up there?"

"Just when I have company like you."

He ruffles her hair. "What does she do—for money?"

"Social Security, I guess. She's old. And there's me. My rent helps her make ends meet she says. She grows things, too. See over there—the garden? Some of it's mine, too. She gave me a plot of ground. I actually planted rutabagas. Can you believe that?"

"You'll be here that long?"

Zoe runs her hand along the railing, searching for a grain or two of dust that needs to be brushed away. "Opal gave me the seeds and told me what to do. It's not hard, really."

"My cousin Cord moved out for two weeks. That was all he could handle. Expenses were too much. It's always more than you think. He couldn't—"

"They're really turnips, you know. A type of one anyway. That's what Opal says. Murray serves turnips." Smoke curls from the tip of her cigarette. Into the air. A foot. Maybe two. And then gone. But the line continues to be replaced by another line and another. She pulls it to her lips, inhales, and then breathes out the smoke in a fast, shapeless gust. "I never had turnips before. Not until I started working at Murray's. They're good with butter and brown sugar. Really. You had 'em? I bet the rutabagas will be even better. At least that's what Opal says."

"But how are you going to make it that long, Zoe? Can you swing it just waiting tab—"

"I'll have to put brown sugar and butter on my shopping list." She turns and narrows her eyes at Reid. She stretches the moment, hoping he grasps what she cannot say. "I have one of those now. A shopping list. Did I tell you? Who would've guessed?" She takes a last puff of her cigarette and stoops to mash the stub in the ashtray she has placed on the porch. She stands and reaches for the door. "C'mon. Let's go in before Carly and Monica eat all the cookies."

He grabs her arm. Holds the door shut. Holds her still against the railing. "Zoe," is all he whispers.

What does he want from her? She can't give it. "I'm okay, Reid. Give the drama a rest. There's cookies waiting. Chocolate."

He doesn't move toward the door. She knows it's more. Not just the room, the knowing or the not, the rutabagas, the rent. It's the needing but not getting, the skimming, the hurry, the take with no give. She has no give for him. What does she have? Only rutabagas. Will it keep him to her?

Keep him in that friend way, not best friend or boyfriend, but friend something, someone who is there. Someone who connects her like a dot to this world.

The possibility of a dirty yellow root is all she has.

"And if you're nice, I'll share my rutabagas with you, too."

The ghost flits between them. The shadowy, shameful one she wishes she could take back like an inhaled breath that never was. He twirls his finger. "Yippee," he says. And he is giving again, Reid again, Carly's little brother, opening the door, plopping in the chair, and reaching for a bag of chocolate cookies.

Cookies, chips, and chopped-up conversations get her through again.

Carlos arrives an hour later. By now, only two taquitos, three cookies, four sodas, a dusting of chips, and three beers courtesy of Monica's older brother are left. No introductions are made. They remember him from Yolanda's party. But a glance from Reid, an odd exchange of glances, and timing that is off tell her she should have prepared Reid in some way. *Shit. It's not like I've been the only one. Get over it.* But then she knows the odd exchange has settled over Carly. She shifts on the window seat, her hand comes up to her mouth, gently, hovering and then back to her thigh. "We gotta go. It's late," Carly says. "I work early shift at the cleaner's tomorrow." They gather up to leave like the bell has rung at school. Only Monica winks and offers a secretive thumbs-up as she leaves.

"Get out of here," Zoe whispers to her.

Carly kisses her cheek. Her expression is serious. "Call me," she says.

"I will." But she doesn't want to explain she has no phone, only Opal's for emergencies.

"Bye, Reid," Zoe calls from the landing. He is already an indistinct lump being sucked up by the darkness at the bottom of the stairs.

"Yeah," he answers.

THIRTY-THREE

"Sorry," he says.

"I'm late," he says.

"I didn't mean to break things up," he says.

But she can hardly focus on the meaning of his words.

He's here.

And she doesn't even know why it should matter so much.

"There's two taquitos left. Better grab one while you can."

"You closing up?"

"It's late."

"Too late?"

They stand awkwardly in the middle of the room. Practically strangers. No table to touch. No pillow to hold. Awkward arms. Legs. No way to cover them. Pretend. Hide. But she remembers the dance. The time they shared at Yolanda's. The time that seemed so right. She reaches for a taquito. Dips it in salsa. Thrusts it out to him. "No. Not too late. It's only"—she glances over to the ticking panther—"midnight. Too late for you?"

He takes the taquito. "No," he says. She gets him a Corona from the refrigerator and takes another Dr Pepper for herself. She doesn't want another soda, but she wants something for her hands. Something to sip in case she forgets how to talk. For the first time she notices the lack of seating in her room. One chair, and the bed. The window seat is so far from the chair, it would be awkward. All these things matter. She sits on the bed and motions to the chair. "Sit," she says. He does.

"So this is your place?"

"No. I just rent it out on Friday nights."

He laughs. "Yeah. Stupid question." He looks around. "Nice," he adds.

"Works for me."

He sips his beer. She sips her Dr Pepper. Her fingers busy with droplets. Wiping. *He should go,* she thinks. *It is late.* The bargain-bin candle burns low. The circle of ceiling light will be gone in another twenty minutes, she guesses. She hates the void. Where does it come from? She has never lacked something to say around a boy before. Her hundred and eighteen pounds of mouth have always been adequate. She jumps up from the bed and grabs his free hand. "Come on. I have a garden. Let's go for a walk." She has released his hand before they even go out the door, but the touch lingers. The clammy warmth. The calluses, knuckles, angles. The largeness of his grip. A two-second exchange becomes a kaleidoscope of memory and want.

"A garden?"

It stops her. A garden. Yes. She has a garden. Bare dirt right now. Furrowed lines. You would never guess. But it will be something. In a few months. Rutabagas.

"Nice dirt," he says as they stop and stare at her small plot.

Nice dirt. She loves that. She knows it is humor, maybe gentle sarcasm, but it doesn't matter. It is shared. And his voice is true like he knows it matters. "It'll be more," she says. "It just takes time. New to me, too. I've never grown anything in my life. Never wanted to. But now that I have it . . ." She shrugs. "I check it every day."

"Trying to hurry it up?"

"Not exactly. More like curiosity, wondering if I really can make something grow."

His arm brushes close to hers. She wants to touch him. Feel him. "Carlos," she says. And with his attention fully hers, she reaches up and pulls his face to hers. Opens her mouth, feels his tongue. His lips molding to her own. She memorizes the touch of his fingers on her throat. The burning. The pulling closer. And then his pulling away and taking a deep, startled breath. She pulls him back again and feels his mouth melt into hers, his hands at the small of her back, until they both have to step back for a breath.

He points through the trees to the black hole that leads through the elms. "What's that way?"

He leads her deeper than she wants to go. Deep as she needs to go. To that place of deeper that never comes. That place she wants. The kaleidoscope turns. Splinters of color, light, darkness, and memory fracture their walk.

I thought you loved me.

You said.

I'll call you. Sure.

It means nothing.

Nothing.

They go deeper into the darkness of the canopy, farther, beyond the elms. To the place the season has changed. Where a carpet of fallen leaves rustles beneath their feet. Where stars can be seen through naked branches.

They stop and press their mouths together again.

She pulls on his back. Presses her hips to his.

She wants to make him happy. She can make him happy. She knows how. She needs him to need her.

She pulls him down so his weight presses on her from above, so leaves press at her back. So a glittering black sky looks down on her. On her.

Special, Zoe.

Stars, Zoe.

She fumbles for his belt, tight between them. He lifts slightly so her fingers can maneuver. Loosen. His buckle is cold in her fingers. Cold. Hard. His breaths are lost in her hair. Heavy. Moving. Lips pressing her ear. Her throat. Hot.

But the buckle is cold.

Stays cold.

Smooth coldness.

Like porcelain.

Cold. Like never-eaten eggs.

Cold.

> *Like.*

>> *Gray.*

>>> *Water.*

She pushes him away. Gasps for a breath.

Touch.

Need.

> Is fractured.

He sits dazed. Tight. Drawing into himself already.

"I'm sorry," she says. "I—"

> but there is nothing to say.

She is not sorry. Not really.

She still wants him. Wants to touch him. Have him touch her. But not, too. Two wants pulling against each other.

"It's too soon," he says. "I don't know what I—"

"No. It's me. Don't say anything."

They go back to her room. Listen to the Everly Brothers on the jukebox. Listen in the dark when the circle of bargain-bin light is gone and all that is left are a few faint ceiling stars still reflecting borrowed light. They lie on her bed and don't touch except for his hand stroking the edge of her little finger. He stays. Doesn't rush. And it all seems too much. Too much for someone like her.

THIRTY-FOUR

"Home fries, not hash!" She slides the plate across the stainless-steel shelf. "Please," she adds. She never says please. Not usually, but today every order seems to come up wrong. Is the cook out for her? Her tips are nosediving faster than one of Kyle's kites on a windless day.

She wipes the counter and sets a new place as she scans the parking lot for Carlos's truck. She hoped he might come. Saturday they met for an early dinner before he had to go to work. Texas cone-droppers, it seems, even have night duties. It was almost like a real date. It was, maybe. They met at the Rocket Gourmet, but he paid for her burger and shake. When he left, there was no kiss, but there was a moment. A hesitant, quiet moment where they seemed to exchange a thought: *I like you. A lot.* The parking lot is void of his battered blue truck. No Carlos. Maybe the shared thought was only in her own needy head.

"More coffee here?" The sleazebag holds up his cup. The cook's bad enough—Zoe can't afford to piss off her best tipper, too. Not today. She forces a smile to make up for for-getting him.

"Coming right up," she says. The pot is empty. It was her turn to brew more coffee and she forgot. Shit. Is all of life out for her today? But it was the orders. All the screwed-up orders. She puts the pot on to brew. "It'll be just a minute. Everything else okay?"

He beams at the morsel of attention she throws him. "Just fine. *Real* fine." He draws words out the way Opal does, but with entirely different possibilities. She endures it, forcing a smile, hoping he might make up for her other meager tips.

"I'm really happy to hear that," she says. "We like to keep our customers happy."

"You do?" His heavy hands shift across the counter. It unexpectedly nauseates her. Like heavy slugs suddenly pricked at the scent of food. Her. She's the entree. She pushes away the shudder. She needs the money.

"Sure. Anything else you need while the coffee brews?" She braces for more.

"Lots. But now's probably not the best time. *If* you know what I mean?"

For God's sake, give it a rest, pal. But she nods. "Yeah."

"You just let me know when," he says, so full of himself. So full of what he has to offer. *Let him know when?*

Like never.

In another lifetime.

When I've been reincarnated into cheese mold.

But she pulls it together. "You bet," she says in a thick buttery voice that has to be worth at least a ten-dollar tip. God, she hopes so. Reid would lay down a twenty for this performance. She forces out the pièce de résistance that would bring down the house. She leans across the counter to boost her cleavage. "You just never know . . . do you? When, that is." *Suck on that one, dirtbag. Enjoy it. It's all you'll ever get.* She smiles and leisurely pushes away from the counter, relishing his flushed face and flared nostrils. *So simple*, she thinks. Like pushing buttons. Pathetic.

She pours his coffee and leaves to deliver other orders, but she knows his eyes follow her, his mind jerks out of control with the first come-on he's probably had in years. He doesn't finish his coffee, and when he leaves he fans his fat wad of bills at the register, like proof that he was deserving of her attentions.

She scoops up his offering. His five-dollar tip is more than she deserved for a simple order of coffee and a short stack. She should be *grateful*. But she's not. It's still not enough to make up for the rest of her tips. Sundays are usually her best day. She counts on that. Tables are fast and friendly. But not this Sunday.

And the worst is not over. She still has to go to Mama's to search for the registration sticker. She's put it off all weekend. She gathers her things and contemplates whether to tip the cook before she leaves. Tip for what? But if she doesn't, things might be even worse next time. She drops two bucks in his tip jar. Two bucks she can't afford to give up but can't afford not to either. He notices and nods. *Don't forget that the next time I work and your thick brain can't tell the difference between a french fry and a stick up your ass,* she wants to say, but instead she ruffles the few dollars in her pocket, smiles, and waves good-bye.

THIRTY-FIVE

"Mama?"

The word sticks in her throat. Barely leaves her lips. The front room is dark. A slice of golden light spills from the kitchen. Another dim glow comes from the hall. The house is unchanged. Newspapers stream from coffee table to floor. Half-filled glasses perch on vacant dusty surfaces, the TV, windowsill, floor, whatever is closest in reach. Blinds are drawn tight, as always, so day and night make no difference. But the smell hits Zoe the hardest. She can almost give it a name now, that rancid mixture of dust, darkness, and surrender. She keeps her breaths shallow, her steps light, so she doesn't sink into it all. She is here for the sticker and nothing more. She has a room now—a room she aims to keep. Zoe knows how to read the quiet. Mama is in bed, but Zoe doesn't want her to stir just the same. She wants to search through the mountain of mail, get the registration sticker, and be gone. How have these weeks changed Mama? She is not sure she wants to know.

She lifts her feet carefully as she walks to the kitchen, but as soon as she enters its doorway, she knows she will not be slipping in unnoticed. Hardly. Grandma sits at the kitchen table, alone, her head resting in her hands. She leans forward, her heavy breasts pushing against the table's edge, her face unseen, only the wrinkled hands expressing anything to Zoe.

Grandma's hands.

Chapped.

Knobby.

Clutching a face Zoe can't see.

Grandma senses her presence and startles upward, her hands dropping to the table, but as she absorbs who has invaded her silence, she settles back into the kitchen chair, large and hard. Her face is expressionless, her eyes dark and circled.

"Where's Mama?" Zoe asks.

"You come with bags, or without?"

"Is she okay?"

"Because I don't have time to waste chewing fat with you. If you're here to stay, that's another thing—"

"Is she sleeping or out?"

"I'll be the first to let bygones be bygones if you—"

"Without, Grandma! There are no bags. There will *never* be bags!"

Grandma bolts upright and strains her voice into a

hushed command. "Keep your voice down, you hear? I don't have these circles under my eyes because I had a good night's sleep! I was up half the night and into the morning with your mama. Her legs cramping, her stomach turned inside out, and then crying and carrying on till she finally cried herself to sleep. Whimpering for the likes of you."

Zoe leans against the doorjamb and breathes out a long deliberate sigh. "Welcome to the world of Mama, Grandma. You just tuned into this station. I've been listening to it for years."

Grandma grunts. "Oh, sure, now that you have your own place you think you know so all-fired much. Well, let me tell you how it really is—"

"No. I know all about Mama, and I don't need to hear it from you. You're so wrapped up in what you want her to be, you don't see what she *really* is." She pushes away from the door and walks to the counter. "I'm just here to pick up my mail. That's it."

Zoe begins shuffling through piles of paper searching for an envelope with a County Tax Office return address. Grandma is quiet. For the first time in Zoe's memory, Grandma has nothing to say. The silence is long and heavy. The words Zoe has spoken have punched the air out of Grandma, and she isn't even sure why. It can't be news. Zoe's shuffling slows as she looks sideways at Grandma, who is leaning back, staring at a kitchen wall that only holds stains and a flyswatter. Lost in the world of Mama. Swallowed up by a kitchen where she doesn't belong, looking smaller than Zoe remembers, not looking like Grandma at all. The mail is forgotten and Zoe stares. She sees flesh and bones of another person. Someone she doesn't know. Who is this woman? *Who is she?* Did she ever have a life outside Mama? Did she ever plan for a spring garden? Did she ever walk past a storefront and yearn for the dress inside? Plan to lose five pounds, just for her? Just because it made her feel good? Did she ever make love with a man? Not sex. She knows there was that with Grandpa—at least three times. But love. On a kitchen table with silverware clattering to the floor. Passionate and urgent, with sweat and screams and laughter. Grandma? Was she ever a woman all her own? And if she was, what happened to her? Where did that woman go? When did she stop believing in herself and start only believing in Mama? When did she lose that part of herself that was truly just hers? How do you lose yourself like that? How long does it take for someone to dissolve away to nothing?

"And you do?"

Grandma has been quiet for so long, Zoe has lost the question.

"Do what?"

Grandma turns in her chair to face Zoe fully. "Think you know so much about your mama. Where'd you get all those smarts from, Beth? From your *daddy?*"

Daddy. Like it's a dirty word.

The quiet was to refuel. Reorganize. Zoe can see that now. No one beats Grandma at strategy. Zoe is silent. She doesn't want to talk about Daddy. Not with Grandma.

"Nothing to say? Well let me tell you about his smarts—"

"Please, Grandma." Her voice is breathy, and she feels the ground she has lost. "Drop it," she says more firmly. "It won't get us anywhere."

"Oh no, I think it will. It'll get some fool notions out of your head that you've been nursing. You brought all this up, so let's clear the air."

Clear air is vulgar and bare coming from Grandma's lips. Needles stab at her throat. "Daddy has nothing to do with this, so let's just leave him out of it."

"You don't know, do you? You don't even remember?" Grandma laughs and shakes her head. "I told your mama that. I told her, but she didn't believe me. I told her you were so sound asleep all you remember was the screaming. Her screaming and throwing your daddy out. That's all you remember." She laughs again.

Zoe throws down the stack of mail in her hands. "I'm going to check the stacks on Mama's dresser." She knows. That will do it. That will change Grandma's gears. That will jerk them out of their determined clear-the-air track.

"Stop! Don't you wake her!"

A point for Zoe.

She walks down the hall, Grandma in pursuit, trying to keep up. Zoe is already opening the door, and Grandma retreats, breathless, afraid to rock the tenuous fleeting world of Mama's peace. Zoe avoids the floorboards that creak. She has them memorized. She has safeguarded the peace more times than Grandma. But in just a second or two it is apparent. Zoe recognizes the soft rumbling breaths and Mama's body pressing into the mattress like she is sewn there. Her slumber is deep. Prescription-pill deep. Drink deep. Pain-free deep. A little peace for Mama. The light is dim, only faint twilight seeps through drawn shades and heavy drapes. But it's enough. Enough to see the beauty of Mama. Enough to see the delicate china doll that is coming undone.

Zoe sits on the edge of the bed, easing down so gently the bedsprings hardly wheeze. The room is different. Grandma has been here. The nightstand is free of glasses and pill bottles, free of rings of dust and clutter. Grandma, trying. Always trying. The dresser is clear, too. Polished and almost attractive. Sheets have been washed. Lampshades straightened. Clothes picked up from the floor. Cobwebs swiped from corners. It could almost pass for a bedroom like any other, if not for Mama. Grandma can change some things, but not all. The picture just over the lampshade still hangs crooked. Grandma didn't bother straightening that. It's Zoe's favorite picture. Mama standing on the courthouse steps with flowers in her hair, smiling at the camera.

Her fingernails are like ten little rose petals spread in a row across her white suit. Her face, happy and young and hopeful. Daddy is standing next to her, not looking at the camera but at Mama. Boyish. Love and wonder filling his face. And Zoe is there, too. Unseen. Mama's tummy still flat. But there. And Mama knew it and was still smiling.

Her hand moves from her lap to lie on top of Mama's hand. "I won all my matches last Friday, Mama," she whispers. "I was the star. Remember what Daddy used to say about the stars—" She swallows against the ache in her throat. "I think you would've been proud. I've come a long way. A couple of years ago, I was dead-last, and now people pay attention when they see Zoe Beth Buckman walk on the court. I even have a cheering section. My own cheering section. Mama? Maybe next Friday you can come." Mama doesn't stir. Zoe knows she won't. "Or another time." Zoe stands and reaches out to straighten the picture over the lamp. She touches the small white inch of glass that is Mama's tummy. *Where did that person go?*

She looks away. *Don't sink in, Zoe. The validation sticker is all you need. Get it and get out. Before it's too late.* She opens the closet door but Grandma has been here, too. There is no mail. Back to the kitchen. Grandma is waiting for her in the hallway.

"This what you're looking for?" She holds up a white envelope. Zoe sees the return address. County Tax Office.

"Yes. Thank you," she says and reaches for it.

Grandma pulls the envelope away. "Whoa. Hold on. Just a minute. These things aren't free you know."

"It's Mama's validation sticker. Not yours."

"Your Mama forgot to take care of it with everything that's been on her mind."

Always the spin.

"So I paid for it. And I guess, well, that *does* make it mine."

Zoe doesn't speak. Doesn't move. Thinks. But there is no strategy. "I need the sticker," she says. "Without it I can't drive, and if I can't drive I can't get to work."

"Oh, Beth. Don't you worry. I'm going to give you the sticker. But with you being such an independent career girl and all, I know you'll want to pay me back for it."

"But I can't afford—"

"Beth." Grandma's face changes. Small wrinkles soften her eyes. The *trying* grandma. The *smoothing-over* grandma. "Let me take care of this. Come home and let's put all this behind us. Start fresh. Come on, now. Be a good girl."

A good girl. She almost could. Except for the lost woman Grandma has become. Except for the lost woman in the photo over Mama's bed. A good girl might come easy, almost, if not for that.

"How much?" she asks.

"Beth—"

"I'm never coming back. Get used to it. Never coming. Never crawling. *Never.*"

216

The hard face returns. Soft lines fold into stone. "Never say never, Beth. I learned that two lifetimes ago. So did your mama. So will you."

"But I'm not you—and I'm sure as hell *not* Mama." Zoe's hands shake. Damn, she needs a cigarette. But she waits.

"Eighty-eight dollars." Grandma holds her palm out.

"Eighty-eight dollars! For a lousy—"

"Twenty percent late fee penalty." Grandma turns and walks back into the kitchen. "Plus toll road fees. Adds up doesn't it? Still want it?"

Zoe pushes past her and grabs her purse from the counter. She counts out ninety dollars and snatches the envelope from Grandma's hand. "Keep the change."

She leaves, slamming the door, hoping it wakes Mama. When she says never, she means never, even though more than half her rent money now lies in Grandma's know-it-all palm.

THIRTY-SIX

The road, too familiar. Too much of the sameness to hold her. It melts away. She glides through Ruby. Glides to then.

Flashes of light.

Screams.

Kyle's startled cries.

She remembers.

Elbows.

Arms.

Clothes flying out the door.

Remembers.

Sharp pieces of memory.

Frozen fragments.

And more.

Grandma is wrong.

She remembers more.

It has come to her piece by sleepy piece—through fog and time.

She remembers. Daddy. Naked. Hovering over her.

Stumbling from the bathroom, blind with vodka, through a door. The wrong door.

Her door.

He never touched her. But she thinks, maybe he didn't know that. Mama's screaming shocked him from his stupor. Mama shoving him through the door. Shoving him to the porch. Beating him. Throwing clothes out on the lawn and screaming to never come back. Never.

He didn't.

Mama saving her and hating her at the same time for everything that happened. Daddy hating himself for what might have happened. What could have happened.

Was it more than he could live with that night?

Or just an accident like the coroner said?

The wondering is the worst. The wondering that eats. Never full, never satisfied, just eating away, a finger, a toe, an eyeball, until maybe it reaches your soul and there is nothing left.

+ *
+

Secrets upon secrets. Secrets that would never be revealed, because Daddy took all the answers with him. Secrets all revolving around her in a distant, untouchable way.

Yes, Grandma.

I remember.

I remember it all.

THIRTY-SEVEN

She swerves into the parking lot of the Rocket Gourmet. Tips at Murray's alone won't cut it now. Not by a long shot. One hundred fifty rent due on Friday and she has thirty-one dollars and a can of pennies. Sunday night is not prime time to be looking for work, but she doesn't have the luxury of time.

"Table for one?" the hostess asks.

"No. Just looking for work. You hiring?"

"Not right now. Not even taking applications, but maybe in a month or—"

"Nothing? Not even busing tables?"

The hostess shakes her head. "Sorry."

"Thanks anyway," Zoe says, and leaves.

She drives to Angelino's Deli, the Buffet Basket in Cooper Springs, and even the greasy truck stop off the interstate, but all that comes of it is an empty gas tank. She conserves her bills and empties out all her spare change onto the counter at Thrifty Gas. The clerk rolls his eyes and begins counting.

"One dollar and forty-seven cents," he says. "That's it?"

"That's it."

She pumps out the gas and then stoops to pick up a dirty penny near her tire—for luck or survival, she isn't sure. But what she would have ignored yesterday she brushes off and slides into her pocket today. She leaves, and when she's halfway down Main she glances at the gas tank needle. It is only just this side of empty.

The drive home is quiet. Ruby is quiet. The streets are empty, the orange glow of the streetlights holding in the silence. Only the oil pump at the corner of Main and Third disturbs the calm. Her car idles at the stop sign. She watches the pump, still so much the horse of her childhood. Her eyes trace the edge of chain-link holding it in. A car behind her honks, and she moves on through the intersection.

+ +
+

She piles the pennies into groups of one hundred. They lie like little hills on her ivy print bedspread. Eleven copper hills waiting to be rolled into rent. The coffee can was backup. Only if she absolutely needed it. She needs it now.

THIRTY-EIGHT

She runs through her mental list, the small circle of maybes in her life. Uncle Clint and Aunt Patsy are still paying off Aunt Patsy's medical bills. It wouldn't be right. Besides, they might tell. Monica never has two cents to her name. Reid? No. Not Reid. Not now.

She can't ask just anyone. She wouldn't. It would make her no different than Mama. But a can of pennies and hope aren't enough now. She winces and presses her stomach. It burns. She ate the last stale chocolate cookie for breakfast this morning and washed it down with a flat Dr Pepper.

But Carly.

Maybe.

Zoe could ask. She loaned Carly money once. It was a long time ago, but she knows Carly would remember. She could ask her at the next break.

She waits on the brick planter outside Math Lab until Carly arrives.

"You didn't call," Carly says.

"Sorry."

"Not a big deal. Things were just weird the other night." She digs with the word "weird," waiting for Zoe to fill in the holes. Zoe tries to shrug it into something else.

"It *was* strange, having everyone over to my own place—"

"No. That's not what I mean. It was Reid. He got a strange look on his face when Carlos came. I asked him about it on the way home, but he wouldn't say anything. What's up?"

Zoe's stomach throbs, and a salty film coats her mouth. "You know he's always had a crush on me. That's probably all it was. I didn't really notice. You have a water bottle on you?"

Carly digs through her backpack. She hands Zoe a half-empty plastic bottle. "You okay?"

"Just my stomach." She takes a swig from the bottle. "And . . . I need to ask a favor. Can I borrow some money?"

Carly doesn't hesitate. "Sure. How much?" She reaches into her backpack again. Zoe puts her hand on Carly's arm to stop her.

"No. I mean a lot of money. More than you've got there. I need ninety dollars."

"Shit. You *really* need money." Carly sets her backpack

down. "Yeah, I can get it to you. I'll have to go to the bank. When do you need it by?"

"Friday."

"You getting a boob job or something?"

"Yeah. Something like that."

"I'll bring it on Thursday."

Zoe is glad Carly doesn't ask what it is really for. The warning bell for first period rings and they part.

The days are getting cooler, but through each class Zoe feels a thin sheen of sweat layering her face, throat, even her wrists. Her stomach is raw. Her concentration is feverish, spiking and melting away.

Carly will come through. Ninety. Thirty-one. Tips.

> *Counseling on Wednesday. A new day. I have to remember.*

Will Carly remember? Thursday, she said.

> *Be a good girl, Beth. A good girl.*

When will Mrs. Garrett call on me? Ever? Will she ever say my name? Cakewalk. Name or no name. Cakewalk. Be a good girl, Beth.

Her stomach must be bloody red by now. She swipes her palm across her forehead and hopes she is not coming down with something.

She stops at Taco Shack on the way home. She has to. Rent or not, she has to stop the burning throb of her stomach. She orders a large cheese quesadilla and a small Sprite to wash it down. The burn continues, and she stops at Food

Star for the cheapest antacids she can find—a tiny roll of the Food Star brand for seventy-nine cents. She eats four of them. By the time she gets home her stomach is better but she is still feeling like shit. Now she has blown four more dollars. Coming down with something might have been better.

She sleeps. It is not even dark yet, but she falls into bed. She melts into the mattress, wants to melt so deeply that she can never be pulled loose.

THIRTY-NINE

"A crush? I can't believe you said that right to my face when you knew!"

Zoe pulls on Carly's elbow. Tries to maneuver her to a quieter place, but Carly yanks free.

"He's my *brother!*"

The day started out so well. After twelve hours of sleep, Zoe woke up refreshed. Almost hopeful. She felt confident enough to buy a Krispy Kreme and milk on the way to school. Everything would work out. But as soon as she stepped into the science quad and came face-to-face with Carly, things began to unravel. What made Reid tell?

"Carly—"

"My brother! My *younger* brother!"

"He's six months younger than me, Carly. That's all."

"And that makes it okay? What was he—*fifteen? Fifteen, Zoe!*" Her voice is shrill, working higher and louder.

Zoe lowers her voice to an angry whisper and glances at the students within earshot. "So are you going to tell the whole school?" She pulls Carly close to the brick wall. "So what! He was fifteen. I was sixteen. Big deal."

Carly retreats, her body softens, like it is tired. Her voice flattens. "It's sick. He's not like *you*, Zoe."

The innuendo of the "you" rolls between them. Zoe can't ignore it.

"What are you saying? I'm some kind of slut?"

Carly is silent.

"Say it!" Zoe says again.

Carly slings her backpack to her shoulder. "I don't think I need to. You already did." She turns and walks away.

Zoe yells after her, still needing to explain, or at least offer a rebuttal. "Give me a break, Carly. It's not like I was his first."

Carly turns. "Don't be stupid, Zoe. He was fifteen. That's exactly what you were."

A long pause fills the air. Zoe tries to gather the words to her, snatch them into an order that makes sense.

Carly adds, "Like I said, he's not like you." She leaves, swallowed up by crowds of students, and Zoe is still trying to find her own words to throw after her.

But there are none.

FORTY

Zoe slides into her seat. Late. But Mr. Ramirez is not like Mrs. Garrett. He doesn't notice. It wouldn't matter to her if he did. Tardiness is other world. A lifetime away, like grounding, curfew, and virginity. Less than mentionable. Zoe only thinks of Carly. Opens her book. Carly. Page 147. Carly. Last night's homework.

Carly.

Carly is a virgin. To her, sex with one guy is monumental. Sex with half a dozen is inconceivable. And when one is her brother it is sure to ice her. That's it, really. That's all it comes down to. Her brother. And that Zoe never told. Carly will come around, though. Zoe is sure of that. But by Friday? Not a chance. And that is what matters right now. Carly would have to stew in her just-right-virgin world for a few days.

Zoe has to move on to basics: rent, money, and how to get it.

She will. But where?

She slips out four more of her Food Star antacids and pops them in her mouth.

Page 148.

Other world.

Right.

FORTY-ONE

Fifth period. Back in Mrs. Garrett's domain, invisible once again. Still ninety dollars short and no prospects. More than ninety if today's tips don't come through. She shifts in her seat, in her other, say-nothing world. She could almost like it for the shutting-out it gives, but the shutting-in is there, too, and the shutting-in is like having no air, like miles of tape are wound around you so you can't move, can't breathe, you can only listen, and listen, and listen. To all the stories you've heard before, but no one will listen to your own.

A hand here. There. Raised. Answering questions. Part of. They go up and down. Hesitant. Sure. Up. Down. Neatly in rows. Like bowling pins, and then one is chosen, and they all fall. Strike! Like a bowling game. Zoe can't raise her hand. She doesn't know the answer. She doesn't even know the questions anymore. She never was part of the game. Not in her other world, her nameless Miss Buckman world.

Shutting in. Shutting out. She moves, nudges, in her small other world.

Counseling on Wednesday. Tomorrow. A new day. Remember. Be a good girl, Beth.

Will Mrs. Garrett call on me? Will she ever say my name?

Come home and let's put all this behind us. Start fresh. Come on now. Be a good girl.

I know the answer. Call on me.

A good girl. Beth.

The bowling pin hands are in order again. Gutter ball. Gutter ball. The pin hands are swept away in disgust. The bowling ball gets meaner, faster. Set up. Pin hands raised. Ready. Strike! All down again.

Strike

      or gutter ball

           down just the same.

Say it.

Say it.

"Say it."

The air is tight. Stretched so taut that all the bowling pin hands are frozen, all the shuffling, bowling ball feet still. No movement because the room is poised. Waiting.

Hoping.

Mrs. Garrett moves from her lectern to the chalkboard, stilted, with caught-off-guard movements like she isn't sure what she heard. Like it would be too good to be true. She picks up a piece of chalk from the tray, poised to write. "The romanticism of Frost's—"

"Say it. Just once."

Tight. Sharp. Measured air and no breaths. Mrs. Garrett turns. Sets her chalk on the lectern and it rolls to the floor, its crack on the tile splitting the air. Another step. And another. And the tilt of the head. "Did you . . . speak out of turn, Miss Buckman?"

"It's only three letters."

Nothing.

"Three fucking letters. That too hard for you? Would the world end if you said it?"

Nothing.

"I know you, Mrs. Garrett. I *know* you."

Eyes to eyes. Connection. Silence.

"Just once. *Try.*"

A pen is picked up. Then a pad. Smooth, barely-there movements, like this moment has been practiced. Waited for. It has. She knows. Zoe Beth Buckman. A cakewalk.

Mrs. Garrett's cakewalk.

She hands the slip to Zoe, and says only word.

"Good-bye."

FORTY-TWO

She sits in Mrs. Farantino's office. Sitting but floating, too. Unconnected. Mrs. Farantino shuts her file drawer a little too strongly. Almost a slam.

"Was it worth it?"

Zoe has no answer. Mrs. Farantino doesn't expect one. She shuffles through papers. Angry. Violation of probation. Suspension from the tennis team pending a review by the counseling team. "Is this what you wanted?" Again, no response is required. She is busy fielding phone calls and other interruptions. Zoe is not the only pain in her life.

"I like you, Zoe. I want you to know that. But you have to do your part, too. There's only so much I can do." She fills out yet another pass for Zoe. Study hall for the remaining twenty minutes of the period. "Was it worth it?" she asks again. This time the phones are quiet and she expects an answer.

Zoe sit-floats in her seat. Above it all. Unconnected. What is Mrs. Farantino asking? Worth what? There is no answer. Zoe's gray other world does not match Mrs. Farantino's neat black-and-white one. But she sees what is happening. What they are trying to do.

"Don't take tennis away from me, Mrs. Farantino. Don't."

"It's done, Zoe. You did it. You made a choice."

When?

When in her whole fucking life did she ever get to make a choice?

She thinks about the connections. Connections that aren't even seen. Not even there. But they are. Like Mr. Kalowatz's sprinklers, barking dogs, and chirping tree frogs. Distant events barely connected by a mist of thought or circumstance. The distance between her, tennis, and Mrs. Garrett. The distance between her and a childhood that wasn't. The distance between her, ninety dollars, and a room she calls her own. The same distance as the sprinklers and barking dogs. There but not there, except in Mrs. Farantino's strangely connected world.

Her thoughts snap clear to Saturday. The next match. Zoe, *the star*. Opal and the Count in the bleachers.

"Don't," she says again, but Mrs. Farantino just sighs and shakes her head.

FORTY-THREE

The rutabagas are sprouting. The earth pushes up in chunks, and baby-soft green peeks through cracks. Zoe hunches like a two-year-old on her heels. Watching. She has never grown anything before. How long will it take? Did Opal say? The last long arms of the sun reach between rooftops to warm her plot of ground, and she checks her watch to make sure she won't be late for Murray's. Even if she kisses every ass three times over at the diner tonight, she will never make enough in tips to meet the rent due on Friday. She fingers a piece of earth away to make growing easier for an emerging sprout. She could give Opal an excuse. She could tell her she was just a little short. She could tell her she'd make it up soon. She could give—

One of the thousand excuses Mama always gives.

Zoe stands.

She brushes dirt from the edge of her skirt and adjusts her apron.

Opal will have her money on Friday.

FORTY-FOUR

"Your windshield's looking just fine, miss."

"Best compliment I've had all day." Zoe pours him more coffee. "That sticker put me out ninety bucks, though. That's a lot of money for a waitress."

"That's a lot of money for anyone. We're all in the same boat." He reaches for his wallet.

You're not in my boat, she thinks. *Not by a long shot. Mama's in my boat. And Grandma. And a sort of best friend who can't even look me in the face and wouldn't loan me ninety bucks to save her life. And Daddy. He hops in now and then, too. That's the kind of stuff my boat's full of, mister. Not you or anyone like you.* But she smiles and accepts his generous tip, because that's her job. Waitresses deliver food and swallow shit—all for the accumulation of small change.

"You take care now, you hear?"

"Yes sir," she says, and forces out a cheerful, "You too."

Tips have been good but tables slow. Murray's diner is

feeling the competition of newer, flashier restaurants sprinkling the outskirts of Ruby. She watches Murray moving between busing tables and studying a menu he has memorized, looking every bit the rat in the snake's belly. This week's special: fish tacos. Fish? In Ruby? But he makes do. That's Murray. She wipes water rings and returns salt and pepper shakers to their holders. She asks Charisse if she can pick up her Wednesday shift. No. Charisse is hoping to pick up more shifts, too. Both the kids need new shoes and her car's transmission is teetering. Zoe wipes the ketchup bottle rim and replaces the cap. She twists so tight the skin of her knuckles whiten, and she slowly slides it back into place near the A.1. Steak Sauce.

Two new parties walk in, and Murray shows them to the best booths. Hope is revived. A few minutes later, more customers arrive, and the evening rush—which is not so rushed—begins. Carlos stops by but doesn't order anything. He's on his way to work. He just wants to say hi. Thursday he'll stop by for a late dinner and talk more, but for now, *he just wants to say hi.*

"Hi," she says, and then he's gone, and she thinks that's probably the nicest thing anyone has ever done for her—except for Opal and the Count cheering for her from the bleachers.

The sleazebag arrives late. Her shift is almost over. He is quieter than usual. His eyes move back and forth across red-rimmed lids, and his large meaty hands rub the top of his thighs like his clumsy come-ons are knotted somewhere inside. He slides into a seat, and though his flaring nostrils and leering eyes still prickle her skin, she is glad that he chooses her end of the counter.

FORTY-FIVE

New day.

She remembers.

She shows.

She settles into her chair. But Group is light today. Not even the counselor comes. She stares at the empty seat across from her that should hold Mr. K, or Mr. Beltzer, or Mrs. Farantino, or maybe someone else from their counseling bag of tricks. Will this count against her? Somehow she thinks it will. Somehow it will be her fault. Somehow at their counseling party to see if she will be able to play tennis, they will count it a no-show. And, oddly, today she wants to talk.

She slides her hands outward across the cool surface of the tabletop until her cheek rests there, too. The air conditioner hums. Her stomach gurgles. There are no Food Star antacids left to calm it. She sits upright and looks at the empty counselor chair.

"So what should we talk about today?

"Your life, Zoe. We want to hear all about *your* life. And your filthy mouth, too.

"*My* life? It's pretty much perfect. Not much to tell. And my mouth? I guess I just got lucky."

She tires of her game and leans back. Stares at the empty chair. Presses against her stomach. Listens to past conversations that speak louder than present ones. Listens to the hum that is always there.

Hush, little baby, don't say a word.

The childhood tune she has sealed away to a dark corner breaks through the silence. The tune Grandma always sang. *Don't say a word.* She remembers the afternoons Grandma was there for her after school, Kyle already in tow, taking her by the hand without explanation, saying today was special, today they would have an after-school snack at her house. Zoe knew what "special" meant and why it was Grandma and not Mama or Daddy picking her up. At ten years old she was light-years from Kyle's oblivious innocence, but she went along. For Kyle's sake she was already going along. And then Grandma would sing tuneless songs around her kitchen to make them laugh while she smeared chocolate frosting on graham crackers and poured cold glasses of milk. Afternoon snacks would grow into late suppers and then borrowing old T-shirts for pajamas. The special time grew and grew until Kyle was cranky and crying to go home. And then Grandma would sing more songs.

Hush, little baby, don't say a word.
Daddy's gonna buy you a mockingbird.
If that mockingbird won't sing,
Daddy's gonna buy you a diamond ring.

But Zoe was not the child Kyle was—she didn't find the song comforting. She wondered at a daddy who only brought home useless gifts and then, as weeks and months went by, the wondering turned—why did Grandma always choose that song? She wished just once the mockingbird would sing a beautiful song and make Grandma be silent.

Hush. Don't say a word. She pushes the song back to its dark corner. But there is no silence. The hum trickles into the chopped-up conversations with Mama that started nowhere and ended up in the same place. Conversations that bled her dry. Conversations that took but never gave. Because Mama needed so much. Because Zoe owed so much. She owed and the debt would never be paid. Owed for growing in a place she didn't belong. Owed for Daddy. Owed for people she never knew and places she never saw. Owed for more than Zoe could ever give. And then, owing nothing because Mama would hold her close and stroke her head. Kiss her. Croon and rock her. Mama loved her. Loves her.

And where Mama's chopped-up conversations leave off, Grandma's controlling ones begin again. Ones that seem to have truth. She only slings hash. She'll never make it. She'll come crawling, and they'll take her back. But there is no "back." No room. No stars. There never has been. There is only the room on Lorelei Street.

Come back, Beth. Start fresh. Be a good girl.

But she is not a good girl. Even Carly says so.

"How's that for starters?"

The chair doesn't answer.

And then there is the constant hum of Reid. Louder now because of Carly. Reid, unbuttoning her blouse. *You're beautiful, Zoe. So soft.* Reid. Touching her breast. Kisses. Tender. Only fifteen. Only looking forward, when she was only looking back.

The air conditioner shuts off, and the silence buzzes in her ears.

She looks at the empty seat across from her.

The bell rings.

Group is over.

FORTY-SIX

"What's wrong?" Zoe flies out of her car. "Is it Kyle?"

Uncle Clint breathes deeply, shakes his head, winding up his way to speak.

"Uncle Clint! What is it?" Zoe fights panic rising in her.

"No, no." He pats his hands in the air like he is putting out a fire. "Nothing like that."

But Uncle Clint never comes to the diner. He has never waited in the parking lot for her before. It's *something*. Maybe "nothing like that" but something worth bringing him to town and interrupting his dinnertime. Zoe tightens, draws in to herself. They stand between her car and the groaning oil pump on the edge of Murray's parking lot. He shifts his feet and rubs his left forearm with his hand.

"I just need to talk to you, Zoe. About keeping this room." She waits, letting her silence percolate through him, letting the pause relay that it's no business of his. He brushes his hand over his thin, closely cropped hair. "You wouldn't do something stupid like quit school, would you?"

She relaxes. "You came here for that?" She is almost touched. Is someone finally concerned about her? "I'm fine, Uncle Clint, and no, I'm not quitting school, and yes, I *am* keeping the room."

"What are you trying to prove, Zoe? Smoking? Moving out? We know you've had it hard, but what does any of this prove? You trying to get back at your mama?"

It's there again. Even with Uncle Clint. It's really not about her or whether she might quit school. It's what it's always about. "Mama? Does *everything* have to be about Mama? For God's sake, Uncle Clint! Can't it ever just be about *me*?"

Uncle Clint moves closer and tucks his chin to his chest. "Don't go raising your voice now, Zoe—"

"I'll raise my voice if I want to!" She throws her hands over her head. "I'll raise it so all of fucking Ruby hears!"

Uncle Clint stiffens. "Your grandma's talking about calling you a runaway. Calling the police so you'd have to go home."

Zoe folds her arms and leans against her car. "Really?" She leisurely draws out the word and smiles. "Whose bluff do you think she's calling? Wake up, Uncle Clint. She won't call. Do you think she really wants the police to see what they'd be sending me *back* to? Come on. Think it through. I have."

She turns to leave.

244

"No matter what, your mama is family. Don't you think you owe her that much? To see her through some tough times? Families—"

"I know, I know! *Families stick together.* Give it a rest, Uncle Clint. What? Have you been going to Grandma's school of guilt? What did she have to do to get you here? Threaten to send Kyle back to Mama?" And knowing the spoken name of her aunt is the period to all conversations, she throws out, "And if families do so damn much sticking together, where the hell is Aunt Nadine? Couldn't she take any more of that *sticking together*?"

He puts his open palm out and sighs. "The keys, Zoe. She wants the keys." With his other hand he gestures over his shoulder. She sees Grandma sitting in his car. An arm hangs out the window with ribbons of smoke rising from a cigarette pinched lightly between fingers of a dangling hand. So comfortable. So sure.

Zoe's fingers curl into her palm. Nails dig into flesh. "When hell freezes over," she says in a low voice. "You lay a single hand on this car and I'll break it." She yanks her purse from the front seat and slams the door. "And I don't mean the car!"

Uncle Clint shakes his head. "I don't know you, Zoe."

She stops and looks full into his face. "Of course you don't. How could you? You haven't had the time." It's said as a fact, almost kindly but it cuts just as deeply. She can see it in the wrinkling of his eyes. She would ease the words, backtrack if she could, because Uncle Clint is a kind man, a soft, quiet man manipulated into something beyond his understanding, but there isn't time, and another glance at Grandma's dangling hand spreads heat like a fire past her temples.

"Go home, Uncle Clint. You've never been part of this. Don't start now." She leaves, working her way across a parking lot that stretches and lengthens with each step. Miles and miles of asphalt because she will never get far enough away. *Never.*

Grandma watches her. Every step. She knows. Grandma holding her with her eyes. Needing her. *Families stick together.* Grandma holding on because she needs Zoe. Holding on because Zoe owes her. So much owing. Owing for dark eyes and dark hair that tie Mama to Daddy forever. Owing for growing in a place Grandma thought she owned. Zoe always owing. But now . . . only just now, thinking there is some other owing, too. Zoe owing herself. Owing herself more than anyone ever allowed. Owing and taking, now. A room is not much. It is not arms holding you. Not a breakfast cooked from scratch. Not a filled seat in a bleacher. Not a phone call or a kiss goodnight. Not much at all.

She pushes open the glass door of Murray's and rolls up close to the wall. Out of sight of Grandma, not yet in sight of Murray. She grips her sides and a jumble of remorse and rage collide somewhere in between. No words form in her mind, only a blind swirl of wants that explode in different directions. It presses her breaths against her ribs in uncontrolled jumps. Jumping breaths like she is seven years old.

"Zoe?"

Her eyes freeze on Charisse's.

"You okay?"

She sucks in, controls her breaths. *Okay?* She hardens her chest, refusing a jerky breath waiting at her ribs. Hardens, so there is no jump at all. Controls, so her words come out smooth. Narrows her eyes to shut away her soul. Zoe, owning her air, owning her space. The hardening spreads upward to her mouth, and a thin smile lines her face. "Of course I'm okay, Charisse. Just breathless from running." She doesn't explain more. She doesn't have to.

She pushes past Charisse, who is still staring, and begins her shift. She works, she delivers, she balances. She smiles, she returns, she wipes. There is nothing else to do. She pushes fish tacos for Murray's sake, though she has never tasted them and never will. She regularly walks past the front window and looks out, keeping her car safe with her eyes. Anchoring it there with her will.

"Miss? Is it too late to change my order to a Philly?"

She doesn't check the order. "Yes. Too late," she answers.

She doesn't keep track of her tips, and at her break she doesn't count them. They are not enough.

They will never be enough.

She sits on a wooden crate in the alley behind Murray's

and draws deep on her cigarette. A remnant of light still brushes the sky a deep royal blue but darkness is seeping into the corners. She hears rustling behind the trash bins. Rats come alive with darkness. She blows out a gust of smoke and listens to their tiny secret sounds. Rustling, rasping, scratching, scratching, scratching. Echoing. They surround her, along with the sour smell of old garbage. The last swath of blue disappears, and the sounds grow louder. Darkness spreads like ink through the alley, and not a single star in the sky shows to make a difference. She sits in the darkness, listening, then mashes the butt of her cigarette in the gravel and returns to finish her shift.

She checks the car first. It sits undisturbed, illuminated with yellow and red neon and the sometime shadow of the working pump. The slashing light sparkles on the chrome, like shooting stars. Stars on a starless night. She pushes away from the window. *When hell freezes over. Ninety dollars isn't that hard to get.*

The evening rush that wasn't becomes the dead calm that is. Murray disappears into the stockroom, and Charisse tops off water for her lone customer. Zoe cleans up the table from her last customers and thinks that Murray will soon let her or Charisse go for the night. She tries to look busy.

And then.

The sleazebag comes in.

Charisse looks up, but Zoe knows where he will sit. Always.

"What will it be for you tonight?" she says cheerfully.

He bites. Encouraged. A smile and tilt of her head. Easy. "What's your *special*?"

"Fish tacos," she says, pouring him some water.

"That *all*?" His clumsy hands paw at the glass, and his lips suck at the rim almost daintily. She notices flecks of white in his thin starch-stiff hair when he tilts his head to sip. He sets the glass down and wipes his mouth like he is swiping foam from a beer. His eyes never leave her.

Her stomach convulses. Only a little. "That's all."

He orders his usual, sirloin with a side of slaw. The steak is tough, and she watches the chewing work a glistening line at the corner of his mouth. A forkful of coleslaw is shoved in alongside the steak and the line grows. She thinks of the fat wad of bills in his pocket. He could have ordered the filet. He could have anything he wants with that much money.

He leisurely finishes his meal, buttering his biscuit slowly, so every surface is covered. It oozes onto his stubby fingers, and he licks them with his lizard tongue. Zoe watches and he enjoys the attention, buttering up another one, this time asking for some of her sweet marmalade to go with it. She obliges.

When he is finished, she adds up his bill and slides it across the counter. He picks it up and pulls a five from his wallet. He reaches to set it on the counter, but she stops his hand with her own. "Are you all talk . . . or some action, too?"

His pupils shrink to pinpoints and his cheek twitches. Two gusts of breaths and his mouth finally works free.

"Plenty of action. I save the talk for after."

"Then save your money for after, too." She shoves the five-dollar bill back to him. "I'm taking off early. Meet me out front in two minutes."

FORTY-SEVEN

A room is not much. It's not a remembered birthday. Not fresh sheets or a greeting at the door. Not a packed lunch or being wakened for school. It's not a hug or interested eyes. It's not a name pronounced correctly, the only name that kept you in this world when you were a peanut to be flushed away. A name that made the angels throw a party. A room is none of those things. And a room is surely not for-giveness. Forgiveness for growing, being, speaking, and breathing. Just a room.

Not much at all.

The motel lamp is dim. A low brown glow spreads a layer of dirty light across planes and edges of a room she can't define. She closes her eyes. A half thought. More of a knowing she tries to get hold of, pin down. *So what. It's not like I'm a virgin.* A half thought with filmy words that she squeezes and turns.

The light is clicked off, and only a sliver of green neon slashes through a draped window.

She thinks on the room. Her room. Not on the musty, colorless carpet beneath her feet. Not on her grease-stained dress falling to her ankles. Not on the meaty hand that cups her breast, or the clammy lips at her neck. The room. She thinks on that.

Beautiful, Zoe.

Soft, Zoe.

Yes, Zoe.

Zoe.

But she doesn't say his name. She doesn't know his name. The room. A bulldog. Space. Air. A thousand stars all her own. The room is what holds her.

It is over quickly. She is grateful for that. *Grateful.* Clothing is gathered. Keys plucked from the nightstand. Her purse tucked back beneath her arm. Soon they are in his car headed back to the diner. A slip of time that lives in a dream world. Hardly there.

He pulls in next to her car and jumps out. He runs around to open her door, but she is already out, rummaging for her keys. He reaches into his hip pocket for his wallet.

"What kind of tip do I owe you?"

She wishes they had taken care of it back at the motel, but she couldn't speak then. Now it is easy. "Ninety," she says. He pulls out a hundred dollar bill and tucks it in her palm.

"Worth every sweet penny," he says. He bends to kiss her cheek, and she hardens her bones into place, forcing them to stay put. It is the least she can do for the extra ten.

He gets in his car and leaves, pulling the air with him, gray exhaust left in its place.

She waits there, the oily fumes holding her. She grips the bill tight so it wrinkles, crinkles, shapes to her fist. *Crinkling, wrinkling.* Her car. She should go to her car. *Crinkling.* But her legs don't move. Murray's neon sign crackles and snaps. The pump groans. It's all the same. *Crinkling.*

But it's not.

What the hell is so different? The yellow sign glows, flattens her into place, and the pump groans. Details swell. But then it's not the sign or the pump at all. It's a glance. A fragment. A second look. Beyond her circle of yellow. Beyond the oily fumes.

She sees him.

Carlos.

Standing at the door of Murray's.

How long has he been there?

A dead weight pulls at her lungs. She forces a step. And another. Until she is an arm's length from him.

"Carlos—"

He smiles. A quick, jerky smile she hasn't seen before. "Just stopped by for a late dinner." His hand brushes through his hair, wipes at his chin, and then is shoved into his pocket to keep it still.

"Right. You told me. I forgot."

"Yeah. Just dinner. No big deal."

His words don't match the stiff movement of his lips.

"Carlos—"

"You don't need to explain."

She doesn't. She is floating, hovering somewhere outside herself. A hollow distance that can't be measured. Far, but as close as skin to skin. She looks at his eyes.

She reads them.

She *recognizes* them.

They are her eyes. Her own eyes.

Her own eyes looking at Mama.

+ *
    +

The hollow distance cracks with the fumbled jingling of her keys. The car. The door. The key. She drives, but she doesn't go home.

FORTY-EIGHT

Black meets black. Moonless sky touches earth and aqueduct. Only low rumbling and a dusting of light on steel beams proves the snaking water is there. Her shoes are gone, kicked loose somewhere in the gravel. A breeze rustles the mesquite, a clattering of leaves, a voice in the blackness.

Never say never. I learned that two lifetimes ago. So will you.

Her foot finds cold steel, and she understands. Can finally root into the feeling. The comfort a cold white bathtub holds. A step. Another. Her feet feeling the way. And voices. Voices twining in with the rumble, the air pushing them up.

What the hell you looking at?

Nothing, Mama. Nothing.

Six inches of steel that can't be seen. Air rushing up her legs. Rushing up. Pulling down. A step. Her arms at her sides. No stretching for balance.

You'll never make it.

No more steps. Just cold steel curling into her toes. Cold smooth steel, numbing, like porcelain. But not enough. Carlos's eyes travel through the black. She sees them again. Sees herself.

Never say never.

Her hands slide up to her arms. She is cold.

Never say never. Grandma is right. She is always right.

The echo hits her in the face, nearly pushes her from the beam.

What Mama wouldn't do for a drink.

What I wouldn't do for the room.

A choking gurgle comes from her throat. She feels the clammy lips at her neck, the paw at her breast. She needs to wash her crawling skin.

What I wouldn't do.

Just like Daddy . . . just like Mama.

Her fingers loosen on the bill still in her fist. Loosen, a cold finger at a time, and the bill flutters like a black butterfly into the rumbling below.

You'll come crawling back.

But she is never coming, never crawling. She can't. There is nothing to crawl back to.

"Zoe," she whispers into the night.

"Zoe," a word thrown to the breeze, wanting to catch somewhere, but her whisper is lost to a moonless night, and there is no one else to hear.

She closes her eyes and takes another step. So black

mixes with light. Up becomes down. Chaos becomes calm. Being becomes not.

Just like Mama.

Just like Daddy.

Never far enough away. . . .

FORTY-NINE

Opal adjusts the For Rent sign in the window. It's been over a week. She's not worried. Someone will take the room. She's read three pairs of eyes, and one leads the rest. She steps back and surveys the room. Zoe's things are gone. The room is as it was before. Exactly as before, except for the stone bulldog. The bulldog had to go.

A car door slams.

"She's here! She's here!" Opal squeals. "I knew it! I could feel it in my bones! I read it in her eyes!" She leans out the window and sees a slight blonde girl standing near a car at the curb. "I knew she was coming! I knew!" She clasps her hands and makes a final sweep of the room.

"Is there anything you can't read in someone's eyes, Opal?"

Opal stops, her caftan lapping at her ankles like a gentle tide. Her head tilts in her comfortable birdlike way and she smiles. "Some things," she says. "Like why you can't take the room off the porch. A little cramped, sure, but the view is fine and the free rent's even better."

"You've already done enough, Opal. More than you know. And I've already stayed here long enough without paying rent. I owe you. I will always owe you."

"No, Zoe Beth Buckman. No owing." She cups Zoe's face in her soft wrinkled hands. "I took as much as I gave. Truly. Now, you can read *that* in my eyes, can't you?"

Zoe looks, reads, nods. "Yes," she answers.

Opal sits on the bed and pats the bare tuftness next to her. Her hurrying is gone out of her. "Sit with me," she says. Zoe does. She has the time. Except for the stuffed pillowcase in her hand, her bags are all packed in her car.

"I'll miss the tennis matches," Opal says. "So will the Count."

"Me too," Zoe says. But in an odd way, she is mostly relieved. It makes it simpler. Being kicked off the team makes her other decisions easier. It's less to hold on to. Almost freeing. She thinks of Grandma, holding so tight, trying to keep together what has already come undone. So much like herself. She smiles. Like Mama. Like Daddy. And now it seems, like Grandma. Parts of them, all a part of her, too. A thought like that would have made her crazy a week ago, but now she can hold it like a harmless bug in her palm.

"You'll be okay, Zoe. I feel it in my bones."

"If your bones say so, it must be true."

"That room is always here, though. Just so you know."

Zoe nods. "And the knowing is enough."

Opal reaches into her pocket and pulls out a large round apricot. "It's a record! One for the books!" she says, and places it in Zoe's hand. "Never had one last till the first week of October before. Hung on just for you. Odder than a June bug in July. What do you make of it? Think it's a sign?"

Zoe turns the apricot in her hand, feeling the delicate velvet of the skin. "I suppose it's fate, Opal. Fate, pure and simple. And maybe a sign, too. A season that's late in coming is finally here."

Opal nods agreement, and they share the silence, a connection like arms holding them together.

The doorbell buzzes, and Opal becomes a flurry once again, shushing the Count, who is bellowing in the hall below. "Quick!" she says as she jumps up and runs out the door, "Should I stick with Opal's Lorelei Oasis? Or should I try something new?"

Zoe smiles. "Oasis worked just fine for me. But why don't you wait and see? It might come to you the minute you look in her eyes." Opal claps her hands together, delighted with the possibility, and nods her good-bye.

Zoe leaves down the outside stairs, her overloaded pillowcase bumping along each step. She takes in each thump, each creak, each scent, each sight, like she is memorizing time, like it is all new and she is overcome with what she might have missed. She glances over her shoulder, back at the garden. The tops of her rutabagas are spiky green tufts now. She won't be here when they are ready to dig up, but Reid said he would come. Was it the drama? Like the final act of a play that made him offer to do it? Or had he forgiven her? He didn't say as much, but she thinks that was it.

She unlocks her trunk and then stops to look down the shaded street, dappled light pocking the sidewalks and cars. Lorelei. A street she never knew existed three months ago. What will she discover three months from now? She almost missed the chance to find out. It's been over a week since she was at the aqueduct, but she can still feel the chill of that night on her arms. She relives it every day. How close. How terribly close. . . .

Voices pushing her but then saving her, too. Her own voice, *finally*, speaking louder than the others. Chopped-up conversations with Zoe as their beginning and end.

Never far enough away.

The possibility came to her. Of her own making. *Far enough*. Pieces of possibility that gathered together in a tight strand.

No matter what had happened, what had brought her to the aqueduct, the wondering was worse. She knows that. Slipping into blackness would leave Kyle with the same wondering that Daddy left her. The wondering that can never be satisfied.

For Kyle. And the wondering that eats. She opened her eyes. She couldn't leave him with that.

And then on the heels of the chopped-up voices there was a whisper on a moonless night, a whisper as crisp as a cold breeze. *Special, Zoe. Stars, Zoe.* Whispers Daddy left her that meant something, too.

Zoe.

> *Full of life.*
>> *You can't flush away life.*

Mama didn't. Mama made a choice.

So could she.

Fate . . . so much pushing it can't happen any other way
> *unless you push back to make it not.*

It was then her arms rose for balance and fear held every cautious step. The night was blacker, the beams narrower, the distance as far as forever, but she worked her way to the other side and fell into the dirt with gulping breaths.

She sat there in the dark, afraid to move. Shivering. Shamed. But alive. Never far enough away, but maybe a place far enough for now.

And then, amazingly, Grandma's chopped-up words last of all as she searched in the dark for shoes she never found.

Be a good girl, Beth. Let's put all this behind us. Start fresh.

Yes, Zoe thought. *Fresh.* Maybe not the fresh Grandma had meant. But fresh in her *own* way. Maybe the kind of fresh Aunt Nadine had to find.

Chopped-up voices. Bits and pieces. All a part of her now. Forever splintered into her for better or worse. But the choosing, the *choosing* is what Mama gave her. Not a peanut growing all on her own, after all, but something of Mama, too.

Bits. Pieces. Endings. Beginnings. And choosing.

She throws her pillowcase into the trunk and looks up at the room one more time. She sees a hand slip the For Rent sign from the window. A momentary fear skips through her, but then she shakes her head. Opal's bones always know. She has to believe that. They always know. She gets in her car and drives the quiet Sunday streets of Ruby to Mama's and parks at the curb just behind Mr. Henderson's pickup. She gets out and pauses at the gate.

The weeds have grown thicker; the summer blooms are all gone. She stares at the house and imagines it with daisies crowding the porch. She imagines a cool, lazy sprinkler and open, breezy windows and a lawn that is almost green. She imagines a young woman sitting on the steps weaving daisy chains into her hair and a man chasing a little boy with a hose.

It used to be a house, she thinks.

You could almost have called it pretty.

The chain-link gate groans as she passes through.

She stops at the steps and looks down at a faded doormat that once said "welcome." She reaches into her pocket and pulls out the last apricot in Ruby, maybe the last one in the universe, and sets it on Mama's doormat. She takes a step back and looks at it. An apricot out of season. Mama loved apricots. Loves apricots. Zoe hopes she sees it.

FIFTY

One hand drapes Kyle's shoulder, and the other opens the door of the Thunderbird. Kyle's shoes scrape the gravel like a puppy, digging to find a safe place. He looks at the overloaded car, bags and pillowcases filling the back seat. "Where you going?"

"Brownsville."

"Where's that?"

"About as far as you can get from Ruby and still be in Texas. It's where Aunt Nadine is."

"You going to live with her?"

"For a while. Maybe. If there's room. But if there isn't, I'll find another place."

"But why there?"

"I don't know. I'll ask Aunt Nadine. Maybe she knows."

But some things have no words, Zoe thinks, no grand explanations that can be puzzled together. They come together in fits of time and circumstance, and the lines melt away until it is simply a new life. Not too far away. But far enough. She won't press Aunt Nadine.

"Grandma says you're running away. Stealing the car and running away."

"Look like I'm running to you? And Aunt Nadine said I could come. Besides, if I was stealing the car don't you think Grandma would be the first one here stopping me? That's just her grumbling. And what did I tell you about that?"

He peels out a slow whistle and says, "Let it breeze right on by."

She rubs his head with approval. "I love you, Kiteman. And if you can, someday . . . you come and see me, okay?"

"Won't you be coming back here?"

She looks down into his light blue eyes, the child eyes she never had. "I don't know. But I think probably not. I think . . . no. Only for funerals or weddings. You getting married soon?"

He laughs and kicks at the ground. She gives him that, the laughter on their parting, to ease his worry. She fills him with it so he can go back to his eleven-year-old life and she can leave with the worries all her own. She gives him that because she can and she always has.

"What's that?" he asks, pointing to the front seat.

"What's it look like? A big, mean, fat-ass bulldog. Buckled in tight because he's my copilot. No one'll mess with us."

"But it's stone," he says.

Zoe looks at the bulldog and nods. "No potty stops, either," she says and erases the last crease of worry she sees in his face. She squeezes his head to her chest one more time before she gets in her car and pulls out of the drive. Gravel rasps under her tires, and Kyle waves madly, waving until he is only a speck on Aunt Patsy and Uncle Clint's green double-wide oasis.

At the stop sign before the highway she opens the glove box and pulls out a map. She spreads it out on the front seat. The paper crinkles—crinkles with a sound she is sure must be the sound of possibility—and her finger slides along a black curvy line to Brownsville.